'You've no—romantic attachments?'

Her hesitation made him look up, and as her eyes met his he saw the sudden cloud that darkened then.

'No.' Caryn lifted her chin and looked challengingly into his eys. 'Have you?'

Adam laughed, taken aback by the direct way she tossed the question back at him. 'Ah—I suppose I deserved that.'

Dear Reader

Can you put the past behind you? Jenny Ashe poses this question in THE CALL OF LOVE, while Sarah Franklin looks at obsessive behaviour in THE WESSEX SUMMER. No claims for a cure, but sometimes help can be found. In WAITING GAME, Laura MacDonald explores the passage from infatuation to love, in a touching story, while Judith Worthy gives us a heroine who married the wrong brother—the right one is *very* right. . . Australian Cam Walters is every woman's dream!

See you next month!

The Editor

Sarah Franklin lives in East Anglia with her husband, cat and 'a very bossy but lovable' dog. Both her daughters, before marriage, worked in medicine, one a nurse, the other an aesthetician. Sarah joined the St John Ambulance Brigade and holds their certificates for nursing and first aid. Writing and researching the medical content of her books takes time; her hobbies include gardening, the theatre, music and painting.

Recent titles by the same author:

AFFAIRS OF THE HEART
GOODBYE TO YESTERDAY

THE WESSEX SUMMER

BY

SARAH FRANKLIN

MILLS & BOON LIMITED
ETON HOUSE   18–24 PARADISE ROAD
RICHMOND   SURREY   TW9 1SR

First published in Great Britain 1992
by Mills & Boon Limited

© Sarah Franklin 1992

Australian copyright 1992
Philippine copyright 1992
This edition 1992

ISBN 0 263 77781 2

Set in 10 on 11 pt Linotron Times
03-9207-57491

Typeset in Great Britain by Centracet, Cambridge
Made and printed in Great Britain

CHAPTER ONE

'SURELY he'll approve of what we're doing here?' Caryn said for the tenth time.

From his wheelchair Peter watched her move the vase of daffodils from the desk to the windowsill and gave her an indulgent smile. 'Of course he will, but I do wish you'd sit down. That's the fourth time you've moved those damned flowers,' he said. 'I don't want this Dr Laine to think I've got a neurotic sister.'

'Mr,' Caryn said cryptically.

'Sorry?'

'*Mr*, not Dr. He's a surgeon.'

'Well—whatever. Your getting worked up isn't going to do our cause much good either way, is it?'

Caryn sighed and forced herself to sit on the edge of the window-seat—sideways, so that she could still sneak surreptitious glances down the drive. 'Oh, Pete, it will be all right, won't it?' she asked anxiously.

'Why on earth shouldn't it be all right? We pay our rent, don't we? All this means is that we'll have a different landlord,' Peter pointed out. 'And after all, he is Mike's cousin. It's not as though he's a total stranger. And from what I hear he's pretty tied up in London, what with his hospital *and* private clinic work.'

'I know.' Caryn chewed her lip anxiously. 'It's just that I have this *feeling*.'

'You and your feelings!' Peter laughed off her fears, but he had learned to respect Caryn's 'feelings' over the past couple of years. She seemed to have an almost uncanny way of sensing impending disasters. Intuition, she called it. Peter privately thought of it as 'Caryn's witchcraft'.

It was one of her famous feelings that had prompted her to ring him on the day of his accident. Her call had come just before he was due to leave for work, begging him not to drive that morning. Impatiently, he had pointed out that it would take him twice as long to get to the hospital where they both worked by bus. 'I know the roads are a bit icy, but they're sure to have been gritted,' he argued.

'Well, I'll go by bus,' she told him. 'If you don't have to call for me you can take more time.'

Standing in the hallway of the house that they'd inherited jointly from their father, Peter had raised his eyes to the ceiling. 'For heaven's sake stop fussing, bossy-boots. You'll be demanding to know if I'm wearing my wellies and liberty bodice in a minute. I'll be fine.' He'd laughed and rung off abruptly, putting her plea for him to be specially careful down to mere sisterly fussing.

Mercifully perhaps he remembered nothing afterwards. They had told him that the articulated lorry had gone out of control owing to a failure in the braking system. It had crashed through the central reservation on the bypass and ploughed head-on into Peter's car. By the time Caryn had reported for duty that morning he was being admitted to Accident and Emergency, unconscious and with serious spinal injuries. It had been the most traumatic day either of them had ever lived through, and had changed their lives totally.

'Look, give me a hand, will you? I'm not meeting this guy in my chair.' Peter made the request not so much from pride as to take Caryn's mind off the coming interview. Reluctantly tearing her eyes off the empty drive, she rose and came across the room to help him out of his wheelchair and into one of the leather armchairs in the comfortably furnished study which they used as an office.

They had been at Wessex House for three months; just long enough to make a cosy little home for themselves in the lodge house and set up their clinic for the treatment of compulsive disorders in the main building.

They had first seen the house when they spent Christmas at Fortunes Cove. Peter had just received a lump sum in compensation for his accident and they had decided to treat themselves to a modest holiday. On Boxing Day afternoon Caryn had pushed Peter out in his chair so that they could explore the village. A sea wind whipped their faces and tugged at their clothes as they set off along the cliff-top from the hotel. Below them an angry green sea lashed the rocks, sending up plumes of spray and forcing them to turn reluctantly inland. It hadn't taken them long to explore the village itself with its one shop, church and quaint thatched inn. But it was while they were walking back to the hotel along the lanes that they had discovered Wessex House.

Through tall wrought-iron gates they got their first glimpse of the square Regency house. It sat snoozing in the winter sunshine, its long windows shuttered and its wrought-iron balcony festooned with naked wistaria branches. Although it was clearly unoccupied, it looked solid and welcoming standing there at the end of a long tree-lined driveway. Caryn remarked on the rosy colour of the mellowed brickwork, but it was the little octagonal lodge house standing sentinel by the gates that really enchanted her.

'It looks just like Hansel and Gretel's gingerbread house,' she said delightedly.

'The people who built it must have had big ideas,'

Peter remarked. 'Lodge houses usually go with stately homes, don't they? This place isn't much bigger than a large family house.'

They had speculated all the way back to the hotel. 'Maybe the lodge was meant to be a kind of eighteenth-century granny annexe,' Caryn offered.

'More like somewhere to stow away a mad uncle,' Peter laughed. 'And by the eccentric look of the place they let him design it too. Did you get a look at the twisted barley-sugar chimney and the mock-Gothic windows?'

Chatting to the hotel manager later that evening, they discovered that Wessex House belonged to a wealthy old lady who had retired to a villa in the south of France two years ago. The place was looked after by her nephew, who was the local doctor. But, excitingly, it was up for rent to anyone who was interested.

'Oh—a car.' Caryn jumped up from her seat, her cheeks colouring. But a moment later she saw that the grey saloon drawing up outside the front door was a familiar one. 'Oh, it's only Mike.'

A moment later Dr Michael Faber put his head round the door. 'Maggie said you were in here. I just popped round to let you know that Adam's been delayed. He had to go into Dorchester this morning to see Aunt Grace's solicitor. He rang to ask me to let you know.'

Caryn resisted the urge to ask why he couldn't have telephoned her. She smiled at Mike. 'In that case why don't we all have a cup of tea to pass the time? I'll go and ask Maggie to put the kettle on.'

'Not for me,' Mike said regretfully. 'I've got a surgery in ten minutes.'

Caryn walked out to the car with him. Mike Faber was the local GP, a widower of forty-five. Until the recent death of his aunt, Grace Laine, the owner of Wessex House, he had been their landlord. Mike had been a good friend to Caryn and Peter since they had become his tenants, but over the past months it had become increasingly clear that his feelings towards Caryn were developing into something warmer. At times it made her a little uneasy. At the time of Peter's accident her plans to marry Richard Bates, a houseman at St Jude's where she had trained, had been postponed. Two months later, when Richard realised how much Caryn's situation had altered, he had arbitrarily broken off their engagement. She had been hurt— much more deeply hurt than she had allowed anyone to see; bitterly disappointed too. And she was determined to keep her relationship with Mike—and any other man she might meet—on a strictly casual level.

'How about dinner later this evening?' Mike asked as they reached the front porch.

'Not tonight, Mike. Pete and I will probably have a lot to talk about after our interview with Mr Laine. Pete pretends he isn't worried about what might happen, but I know he's as anxious as I am underneath all that bravado.'

He smiled understandingly. 'Of course.'

As Caryn looked up at the tall man with his kindly blue eyes her heart softened. Sometimes she almost wished she could fall in love with him. Mike would never let her down as Richard had. She always felt so *safe* with him; he was kind and patient and gentle. Impulsively she reached out to touch his hand.

'Thanks for everything, Mike,' she said softly. 'We could never have managed without you. Since we came to Fortunes Cove you've been a tower of strength.'

He lifted his shoulders in a helpless gesture. 'I only wish I could do more, but as you know it's out of my hands now. Aunt Grace left the house to Adam, and now its future is up to him.'

'Our future too, unfortunately,' Caryn sighed. 'He's said nothing to you since he arrived, then?'

'Not a word. Adam always did play his cards close to his chest. Anyway, we were never all that close. He's quite a lot younger than me.' Mike grinned goodnaturedly. 'I dare say he thinks of me as an old fuddy-duddy, buried alive down here in deepest Dorset; I dare say he pictures me handing out pills and potions for gout and croup while he performs minor miracles of orthopaedic surgery in his London clinic.'

Caryn frowned. 'He sounds awful.'

'Oh, no, he isn't,' Mike smiled reassuringly. 'I'm sure you'll like him. Women usually do,' he added ruefully. 'Anyway, don't worry—I can't see any possibility of him wanting to live here. I'm sure he'll be only too happy for you to stay on and continue your good work.'

'I wondered if he might want to sell,' Caryn said, voicing her worst fears.

He shrugged. 'If he did, could you manage to buy it?'

'We spent most of Pete's compensation on the improvements,' Caryn said thoughtfully. 'Of course, we didn't get a bad price for the house Dad left us, but buying a place the size of Wessex House would take some thinking about.'

He patted her shoulder. 'I shouldn't worry about it. It's my guess that he'll be pleased to have someone like you and Peter taking good care of the place.'

'I hope you're right.' Caryn looked at her watch. 'You'd better go, Mike. Mustn't keep your patients waiting.'

After another half-hour of waiting, Caryn sent Peter off to take his rest. She normally insisted tht he took an hour's rest immediately after lunch. Today they had rearranged their whole afternoon to accommodate Mr Adam Laine. Maggie Cookson, their part-time house-keeper, who usually went home in the afternoons to attend to her invalid husband, had stayed on specially to serve them tea. Now it looked as though none of them need have bothered, she told herself irritatedly.

Having settled him in his room and packed Maggie off home, Caryn walked out into the spring sunshine. As the afternoon's group therapy session had been cancelled she might as well use the time doing a bit of gardening. She had already changed into an old pair of jeans and a sweatshirt, and now she fetched her wellingtons and a spade from the potting shed. If Mr Laine arrived now, which looked doubtful, he could damned well take her as he found her. She began to dig furiously in the herbaceous border under the office window, working with a vigour born of frustration. It was bad enough being kept in suspense about their future, but if there was one thing Caryn hated it was time wasted. It looked as though this afternoon was going to be a complete write-off.

At the same moment that Caryn began to attack the herbaceous border Adam Laine was driving his car with similar frustration through the Dorset lanes. He was intensely annoyed. His aunt's elderly solicitor had kept him waiting for more than three-quarters of an hour in a stuffy waiting-room, and then mislaid a letter his aunt was supposed to have left for him, delaying him for another fifteen minutes while his secretary searched for it. 'Old Godfrey Haversham might have been a friend of Aunt Grace's, but he's definitely past it,' he muttered to himself as he glanced at the dash-board clock.

He turned in through the gates and zoomed up the

drive of Wessex House, sending a shower of gravel flying into the shrubbery. Parking his bright red Porsche in front of the pillared porch, he ran up the steps and rang the bell. But as he waited in vain for his ring to be answered his already overstretched patience grew shorter. He rang again, this time leaving his finger on the bell and listening as the insistent peal shrilled out somewhere in the deepest regions of the building. To his fury no one came. He stepped back to glare up at the windows. What on earth was the matter with these people? They wouldn't last a day in London with their lackadaisical ways. He'd set himself a tight schedule. If he didn't attend to this matter today all his careful plans would be shot to pieces. It really was too bad. He set off angrily, striding purposefully round the side of the house in search of some sign of life.

At first he thought the place was deserted, then he saw a lad with scuffed jeans and hair like a bronze chrysanthemum grubbing about in the flowerbed under the study window.

'Hi—hi there, *boy*. Is Mr Dean at home?'

Caryn looked up, her face pink at this arbitrary and slightly insulting form of address. 'I'm afraid he's resting at the moment.' She pulled off her gardening gloves and straightened up. 'I'm *Miss* Dean, actually. Maybe I can help.'

It was Adam's turn to flush as the striking amber-green eyes challenged him. '*Oh*. I'm sorry, I didn't see. You had your head down and. . .'

'I take it you're Mr Laine.' Caryn dug her spade into the earth with a vicious jab. 'You'll have to excuse me if I don't shake hands.' She rubbed her palms on the seat of her jeans. 'We'd quite given you up. But if you'd like to go round to the front I'll be with you in a minute.' As he walked away she took in the well-cut charcoal-grey suit, gleaming white shirt and handmade shoes, immediately comparing them to Mike's well-worn tweeds. At first sight it would appear that Adam Laine was just about as different from his cousin as he could be. In fact, a real smoothie, by the look of him. She hated the type; they usually considered themselves to be God's gift. But as she went off to the shed to discard her wellingtons she reminded herself sternly that she was in no position to allow herself the luxury of getting on the wrong side of him.

Five minutes later she found him waiting for her on the front porch.

'If you'd like to wait in the office I'll get my brother,' she said, pushing the door open for him. 'He's down at the lodge. We live there, you see.'

'Oh.' He sighed, glancing at his watch with ill-concealed impatience. 'Will it take long? I seem to have been waiting around for most of the day.'

'And so have *we*, Mr Laine,' Caryn told him. 'Actually, we changed our whole routine to fit in your appointment. My brother will be a quick as he can, but I believe you already know about his disablement. He walks only a few steps, and with difficulty.'

Adam had the grace to look shamefaced. 'Yes, of course—I did know. I'm sorry to appear impatient. It's just that it's been one of those days—nothing but delays.'

Caryn's eyebrows rose slightly. 'I know the feeling,' she told him succinctly.

'I've had a tiresome day and I've kept you waiting around too, so I'm sure you'd like me to come straight to the point,' Adam said when they all three faced each other across the office desk ten minutes later.

Caryn and Peter murmured their assent, carefully not looking at each other.

'Of course, I wouldn't expect you to vacate the

property immediately, so shall we say by the autumn? In other words, six months' notice. I believe that would be more than fair, don't you?'

There was a stunned silence and Peter and Caryn glanced at each other. As always Peter's face revealed nothing, but one look at Caryn's eyes told Adam that his news was far from welcome.

'Do I—take it you'd like longer?'

She shook her head. 'Mr Laine, perhaps you don't realise that we've sunk a large chunk of our savings into this venture.'

His eyebrows shot up. 'Oh? I was under the impression that you were employed by a charitable trust.'

'That's correct, but it only pays our salaries. We've spent quite a lot on the house out of our own pocket.'

'Nothing structural, I hope?'

'No.' Peter spoke up for the first time. 'Mainly simple things to make life easier for me; simple but costly—a few wheelchair ramps, strategically placed handrails. We turned what used to the butler's pantry into a ground-floor bathroom and installed showers to save on fuel bills. Then there's the work we've had done in the lodge, of course.'

'That was in quite a bad state,' Caryn put in. 'We've made our own home there, you see. Then we've put extra power-points and more facilities in the bedrooms here in the house,' she went on, 'for television, tea-making—that kind of thing. We only employed reliable workmen, and of course we've done nothing without Mike's—Dr Faber's approval.'

Adam noted the use of his cousin's Christian name. 'Well, all that seems perfectly reasonable,' he said mildly. 'Naturally I'll reimburse you for any out-of-pocket expense you've incurred. Actually, you've done me a favour. I'd have needed to do most of the things you've mentioned myself anyway.'

Caryn stared at him. '*You* would?'

'Yes.' Adam leaned back in his chair. He looked relaxed and pleased with himself. 'I plan to turn Wessex House into a convalescent home for my patients, you see.'

'The patients from your *private* clinic, I take it?' Caryn asked pointedly. 'The one established by your late aunt?'

'You're very well informed.' The smile remained on Adam's face, but his dark grey eyes flashed with a hint of resentment. This girl with her insolent green eyes seemed to have wormed most of his private business out of Mike. He planned to speak to him about it.

Sensing the hostile atmosphere between the two, Peter touched his sister's arm. 'Caryn,' he said quietly, 'Wessex House belongs to Mr Laine now. If he wants us to leave we have no choice but to agree.' His heart sank as she turned towards him. He knew that determined look of old.

'I'm not at all sure that you're right there, Peter,' she said icily. 'Dr Faber gave us to understand that we could rent the place indefinitely. We'll have to consult our solicitor and find out what the position really is.' She directed a look of cool determination at Adam Laine. 'A lot of people have already been helped here, Mr Laine,' she said. 'And we have many more on our waiting-list. As a doctor are you really prepared to dash their hopes?'

He smiled back at her with equal cool. 'I'm sure you'll find other accommodation, Miss Dean. Maybe somewhere even better than this. And as your brother has pointed out, Wessex House does now belong to me. Any agreement you may have made with Dr Faber is surely null and void.'

'Well, as I said, we shall have to take legal advice on that,' Caryn said stubbornly.

Adam swallowed his irritation. 'And I'm sure you'll
sympathise with the fact that I do have my own, equally
deserving patients.'

Caryn said nothing, picturing his idea of 'deserving
patients'—victims of skiing accidents, no doubt, and
others with limbs carelessly injured in expensive leisure
pursuits.

'Can we get you some tea?' Peter said placatingly.
'If you've had a trying afternoon you're probably ready
for some.' He propelled himself towards the door.

'Oh—please, don't trouble yourself for me.' Adam
sprang up to open the door.

'It's really no trouble. I can manage perfectly.'

Adam sat down again quickly as Peter let himself
out of the room. He knew from experience that it was
important for disabled people to be allowed to prove
their independence. It was just that he'd had a hell of
a day, and now this exasperating girl. . . 'I wish he
wouldn't,' he said. 'I really don't want——'

'To be beholden to us?' Caryn suggested with a
raised eyebrow. 'There's no need for you to feel like
that. We'd asked our housekeeper to stay on this
afternoon so that we could make you welcome, but I
had to let her go at half-past three. She has an invalid
husband, you see. It didn't seem fair to keep her
hanging around.'

Again *that reproachful tone and look*. Adam swallowed a tart remark. 'I was delayed at the solicitor's,'
he said, controlling his voice carefully. 'There was
some wretched letter missing. It really wasn't my fault
I was late. I hate unpunctuality.' He frowned. 'And I
did telephone. Didn't you get the message?'

'Eventually,' she told him. 'Dr Faber is a busy man
too. And we *are* on the telephone here.'

'I couldn't remember the number, and there was no
directory in the phone box.' Adam broke off. Damn it,

why should he have to explain himself like some errant
schoolboy? This was *his* house. All the same, he could
see that he was dealing with a very determined lady.
Better to tread gently. He wasn't sure whether the
Deans' arrangement with his cousin was contractual or
merely verbal. Mike wasn't the world's best businessman, and it was clear that this girl had wound him
around her little finger. He wasn't at all sure of the
legal position himself either. He wanted to kick himself
for not asking old Haversham while he had the chance.
Maybe it would be diplomatic to try a more sympath-
etic tack—ease this spikily defensive female off her
high horse a little. He cleared his throat and forced his
facial muscles into a smile.

'I'd like to hear all about your project here, Miss
Dean.'

'You mean you'd like to look round?' She didn't
quite add, To see if we've done any damage, but the
flashing green eyes said it all.

'That wasn't what I meant at all. What I had in mind
was—dinner.' He said the word impulsively as it
popped into his head. 'Yes, dinner.' Somewhere quiet
and relaxing where we could talk.'

'The three of us, you mean?' Caryn looked at him,
her head on one side, reminding him more strongly
than before of a bronze chrysanthemum.

'Naturally. What else?'

She seemed to relax slightly. 'Well, that's very kind
of you. We'll ask Peter when he comes back—which
reminds me, I'd better go and help him with that tea,
if you'll excuse me for a moment.'

Half an hour later, as they waved off the red Porsche,
Peter looked reproachfully at his sister. 'You needn't
have been quite so abrasive,' he remarked. 'I'd have

thought this was an occasion to exercise your consider-
able charm.'

Caryn pulled a face. 'I didn't *feel* charming,' she
said. 'I hate that over-confident, smug, *oily* type.'

Peter shook his head. 'Oh, come *on*. The poor bloke
wasn't that bad. And all he wants is the use of his own
house. . .'

Anguish filled her eyes. 'Oh, Pete—after all our
work. Just when we were beginning to get results, he's
chucking us out. I can't bear it.'

'He's not exactly chucking us out. Look at the
positive side,' Peter urged. 'We've got all summer to
find somewhere else.'

'But I don't *want* to find somewhere else,' Caryn
protested. 'I love this house. It was sad and neglected
when we found it, and we've made it live again. I know
it's silly, but I feel it loves us too. We've made it feel
wanted again.'

Peter laughed. 'I wish Laine could hear you now.
He'd never recognise the hardboiled cookie who froze
him to death with her eyes ten minutes ago.'

'Did I really?' Caryn sighed. 'I'll try to be nicer to
him this evening. It's just that it means so much to me.
And the thought of all his pampered rich patients
luxuriating here—it just makes my blood boil.'

'Well, try not to let it boil over this evening,' Peter
said. 'I only wish I could join you, but we really can't
both be out at the same time.' He frowned at her. 'I
can't think why you didn't tell him that.'

Caryn said nothing. She'd had her own reasons for
suggesting a threesome. Looking out of the window,
she saw a group of their clients walking up the drive.

'Oh look—it's the gang back from their walk. And
Maggie's with them. I'd better go and help her start
dinner.'

* * *

Caryn had plenty of time to think as she helped Maggie with dinner. Pete had a point. There was no point in antagonising Adam Laine. If he had made up his mind about taking over Wessex House there was very little they could do about it. He had said he wanted to hear about their work—well, all right. She'd go all out this evening to convince him of how worthwhile it was. Maybe—who knew?—she could soften his flinty, avaricious heart into letting them stay.

After the meal she went down to the lodge to shower and change, leaving Peter in charge at the house. Peering at her reflection in the mirror, she sighed and shook her head. She didn't really bother much about her appearance nowadays. Her coppery-brown hair was cut once a month in the short spiky style that accentuated her high cheekbones and made her eyes look even larger. She rarely wore make-up any more, and she lived mostly in tracksuits or jeans and sweatshirts. She pulled open her wardrobe door and thoughtfully surveyed the contents. There were still some sophisticated things left from the old carefree days at St Jude's. Richard had liked smart restaurants and the occasional extravagant evening out at a nightclub. He'd loved to spend his time off at ritzy hotels and his holidays in fashionable Continental resorts. Luckily he had the money to live up to his expensive tastes. Caryn sighed reminiscently. It had been a totally different world when she'd been at St Jude's—before Pete's accident. Yet oddly enough she didn't miss the parties or the dressing up at all. The work she and Peter had started here at Wessex House was so rewarding that whole weeks went by nowadays without her thinking about Richard, and that was something she'd thought would never happen.

She pulled out a pair of skin-tight black velvet ski pants and a striking satin evening jacket in a harlequin

pattern of brilliant jewel colours, smiling mischievously
as she held it against herself. Shock tactics might be
effective. She hung them on the outside of the wardrobe. Might as well be hanged for a sheep as a lamb.

She coaxed her unruly hair into a halo of soft petals
and applied a subtle make-up to complement the bright
colours of the jacket. Then, to complete the outfit, she
found a pair of strappy sandals with impossibly high
heels. She grinned at her reflection in the mirror as she
applied a dash of perfume—the last of a bottle that
Richard had bought for her in Paris. Good job Pete
isn't here to see me, she told herself impishly. I've a
feeling that he'd think this version of Caryn Dean a
darned sight more dangerous than the hardboiled
cookie with the freezing eyes.

When she answered Adam's ring at the lodge doorbell
he hardly recognised the transformed figure standing
before him. But he was well schooled in concealing his
feelings and managed a casual nod.

'Good evening, Miss Dean.'

She held the door open. 'Oh, Caryn, please. If we're
to dine together we can hardly go on being so formal.'

'Of course not. Please call me Adam—Caryn.'

She grinned. 'Thanks, I will.'

He looked approvingly round the tiny hallway. 'I
must say you've made this old place look nice.'

The floor was of polished boards covered by a
brightly coloured Indian rug. The walls were painted
white, making a perfect background for a set of framed
watercolours.

'I like the pictures.' Adam stepped closer to inspect
them.

'Thanks. It's Peter's hobby. He's rather good, isn't
he?'

'He certainly is.'

'Come into the living-room,' Caryn invited. 'Perhaps you'd like a sherry.'

Adam smiled. 'Just a very small one, as I'm driving.' His eyes swept admiringly round the room with its odd corners and niches. Caryn had made good use of them, using them to display her collection of glass and porcelain on glass shelves. Chintz curtains hung at the Gothic mullioned window that looked out on to the drive and caught the evening sun. Again, the walls were painted white, which gave an impression of light and space. Under the window stood a deep buttoned chesterfield, covered in the same faded chintz as the curtains, and a Chinese rug in similar pastel shades lay before the stone fireplace, flanked by comfortably worn armchairs.

'I can see what you mean about this place,' Adam remarked as he took the glass Caryn handed him. 'When I was a kid I used to play here. It was empty then, dark and creepy. I can't remember a time when it was occupied. Later it fell into an even worse state. This is a positive transformation. Congratulations.'

'We've often wondered about it,' Caryn said, sipping her own drink. 'The house doesn't really seem large enough to warrant a lodge house.'

'It wasn't here originally,' Adam told her. 'Early last century it was used as a vicarage. The incumbent, who was quite well off, had a large family, so he had this built as servants' quarters.' He looked down at the wide, polished oak boards that made up the floor. 'Did you have new floors put in?'

She laughed. 'Heavens, no. We hired a sander and did them ourselves.'

'Your brother and you?'

'Yes. Peter can do quite a lot if there's someone around to help him. We did all the decorating ourselves too. The only tradesman we employed was an electrician. Better safe than sorry when it comes to electricity.'

'You must have worked very hard.'

'Yes, we did.' She looked at him enquiringly. 'If you've finished your drink shall we go?'

'Oh—yes, of course.' He'd been looking at her curiously, trying to make up his mind. She seemed to have changed totally from the girl who had got so irritatingly under his skin this afternoon. And it wasn't just the clothes and make-up that transformed her. There was some other elusive little piece of feminine wizardry. Then, as she picked up her bag and turned towards him, he knew. It was the smile. The ice in the flashing green eyes seemed to have melted. Their expression was softer—almost sunny. They were more amber than green this evening—amber-gold with flecks of. . .

'Is everything all right, Mr Laine—Adam?' She was looking at him enquiringly.

He swallowed and drew himself up sharply. 'Perfectly. Shall we go?'

CHAPTER TWO

'MIKE tells me you treat people with compulsive food disorders.'

They were seated in the restaurant, their food ordered. Caryn leaned back, sipping her Campari and soda. She was enjoying herself. She was impressed by Adam's choice of restaurant: the As You Like It had a name for its fine cuisine and wines. She and Peter had passed it often on their travels and often wished they could afford to try it. Eating out at good restaurants was one of the things they both missed. Peter would love it here, she told herself as she looked round her. Richard too would have appreciated the relaxed atmosphere and the quietly elegant décor. It was odd, after all this time, how she still caught herself applying his standards—remembering his likes and dislikes.

Out of sheer devilment she had ordered the most expensive dishes on the menu. If she was going to be put out on the street she might as well go in style. Anyway, Adam Laine looked as though he could well afford it.

'I take it that covers a number of things?' He was looking at her enquiringly, and she reminded herself that they were supposed to be here to talk about the clinic.

'That's right. Anorexia, bulimia, compulsive eating. . .' She broke off at the look of faint distaste on his face. 'They *are* very real illnesses,' she told him. 'Ones whose symptoms mask much deeper conflicts. The Gregory method treats on a self-help initiative basis.'

Adam looked sceptical. 'I don't think I've heard of this—what did you call it—*Gregory* method?'

'Lisa Gregory is a psychotherapist. Peter and I got to know her after his accident, when he was recovering at the rehabilitation centre. It's a method she devised herself. When she knew that I'd done some psychiatric nursing she asked me if I'd like to work with her. I'd had to give up my job at the time to look after Pete, you see.'

Adam nodded. 'It must have been a very worrying time for you.'

'It was. It began to look as though neither of us would ever be able to earn our living properly again. When Pete was fit enough Lisa invited us to move in with her at the clinic she runs in Yorkshire. We were there for six months, studying her method and gaining practical experience. At the end of that time she suggested that if we could find suitable accommodation in the south she'd like us to open and run a clinic for her here.'

'You must have been very grateful to her.'

Caryn looked up at him, her colour deepening. 'I'm sure it wasn't done out of *charity*.'

'I'm not suggesting it was—just that it must have seemed like a heavensent opportunity for you.'

'Lisa seemed to feel that the three of us meeting as we did was fortuitous all round,' Caryn said stiffly.

At that moment the waiter appeared and placed their starters in front of them. The tension eased a little and Caryn reminded herself firmly that she was Adam's guest. All the same, his patronising attitude still rankled.

'So tell me a little about this revolutionary method,' he invted.

She took a spoonful of her avocado cocktail and savoured it thoughtfully. Was it her imagination, or

had he put a slight accent on the word *revolutionary*?
'Most of our clients are sent to us after they've been in
hospital,' she told him. 'Hospitals still treat only the
symptoms of compulsive disorders. Naturally they're
concerned only with preserving the patient's life. We
try to uncover the underlying cause of their problem
and help them to help themselves.'

'And how do you go about that.'

This time she was sure of it. Yes, the dark eyes were
lazily amused—*definitely*. Clearly he thought Lisa
Gregory was some kind of quack. She had the distinct
impression that he was deliberately doing his best to
make her lose her cool, and she was equally determined
not to fall into the trap.

'In many ways,' she said calmly. 'Group therapy
helps a lot. Through that we learn what might work
best for individual clients, because no two people are
the same. There's no set pattern of treatment, no drugs
or medicine.'

'How long do your patients—er—*clients* stay?'

'It varies. A week—two; sometimes they come for
weekends. Very rarely we get a long-term one.'

'I see. And how many staff do you employ?'

Caryn frowned. It was getting more like an interrog-
ation by the minute. 'Maggie, our housekeeper, that's
all. Clients share the domestic work on a voluntary
basis. Everyone mucks in and helps out—that's part of
the therapy. And clients who no longer need regular
therapy often come just for the odd weekend to help
us out—because they enjoy it. We have one regular,
Fred. He turns up almost every weekend.'

Adam looked surprised. 'I thought that people with
these kind of problems were always female.'

'The term "compulsive disorders" covers many
things. Fred's a reformed alcoholic.'

'Really? Regular little miracle-workers, aren't you? Do you cure smokers too?'

There was a sudden sharpness in his voice that made Caryn look up. 'We don't claim to *cure* anyone, we help clients to discover the underlying reasons——'

'I know, I know.' He waved a hand dismissively. 'You've already told me.'

Caryn bit the inside of her lip, determined to keep her temper. 'Smoking might be unhealthy and anti-social, but it isn't in the same category as drug addiction,' she told him.

His eyebrows rose. 'You take addicts as well, then?'

'Occasionally.'

'It all sounds most intriguing.' There was a long pause as the waiter removed their empty plates and put the main course before them. By the time he had gone Adam seemed to have recovered his composure. 'Tell me, what made you choose Wessex House?'

'We were in Fortunes Cove for Christmas. We weren't actually looking for a house at the time, but we fell in love with it on sight. It seemed—it *is* so exactly right.'

'But any other country house would serve equally well, surely?'

'Country houses to rent aren't all that easy to find,' said Caryn.

'Especially at the kind of rent you're paying.' Adam glanced up at her.

'We pay what we were asked to pay,' she retorted. 'And you can't deny that we've improved the place.'

'No, I grant you that.'

She glanced up at him daringly. 'If you don't mind my saying so, it was beginning to crumble from neglect when we took over.'

'Ah, but I hadn't inherited it then, had I? I can promise you that things will be different from now on.'

Adam smiled disarmingly into her eyes, and the blush that deepened her colour this time was not the product of her irritation.

He looked at her, noticing for the first time that she had a sprinkling of pale gold freckles across her nose. At their first meeting this afternoon he had thought her plain, but now, with her eyes shining and her cheeks blushing rosily, she looked quite different. 'Let's talk about something else, shall we?' he suggested. 'Your brother's very courageous. What was his job before his accident?'

'He worked in hospital administration.'

'So he's doing much the same—on a smaller scale.'

'Yes.'

'You seem close,' he commented.

'We are. Our mother died when we were at school, and Dad died soon after Pete went to university. After that we only had each other.'

'You shared a house—or flat?'

'For a while—the family house that we inherited when Dad died. We lived there together until I moved out to live with my—with a friend.'

Their eyes met, hers daring him to ask the obvious question.

'So you still have the family house?' he queried.

'No. We sold it to move down here and set up the clinic.'

'If you don't mind my saying so, that was rather a bad move,' he said.

'I dare say. But none of us can foresee the future, can we?'

He chose not to take her up on the remark, concentrating instead on his food. 'You've no—romantic attachments?' he asked after a pause. Her hesitation made him look up, and as her eyes met his he saw the sudden cloud that darkened them.

'No.' She lifted her chin and looked challengingly into his eyes. 'Have you?'

He laughed, taken aback by the direct way she tossed the question back at him. 'Ah, I suppose I deserved that. No, none for me either, at the moment. Not serious ones, at any rate.'

Caryn looked away. He was the type who played the field; she'd seen that from the first. And Mike had hinted that he was popular with the opposite sex.

A small group of musicians had begun to play now. Seeing Caryn push her plate away, Adam asked, 'Would you like to dance?'

She was about to refuse, then she changed her mind. The evening wasn't turning out quite as she had intended. His probing questions and the dark eyes that bored into her like lasers had made her more uncomfortable than she cared to admit. Suddenly the brash image she had tried to achieve was no longer stout enough for her to hide behind. Like it or not, she was not the same person she had been when she had last worn these clothes, and right at that moment she badly needed some kind of diversion. She flashed on her brightest smile, determined to play her part to the last. 'Why not?'

Once on the dance-floor she decided to turn the tables. After all, she had answered all *his* questions. Why shouldn't she ask him some? 'Tell me about your plans,' she said. 'I expect you've something much more upmarket in mind. A swimming-pool, saunas, a Jacuzzi or two? There's plenty of room for a tennis court at the back.' But when she looked up at him she found he wasn't smiling. In fact, he looked quite annoyed.

'I haven't got to the planning stage yet,' he said dismissively. 'There are other, more mundane things to attend to first. When I need some ideas I'll let you know. You've obviously got a fund of them.'

He was a good dancer, holding her close enough to guide her steps so that she found dancing with him easy and relaxed. His body was strong and firm-muscled without an ounce of spare flesh, and she guessed that he kept himself in shape, perhaps with a daily work-out at a gym or some form of regular sport.

'Do you play squash?' she asked him.

He looked surprised. 'Yes, every day when I get the chance. I like swimming and wind-surfing too. It's one of the things I'm looking forward to. I'm planning to spend most weekends at Fortunes Cove while the work on the house is in progress. I love the sea.'

'Me too. When Pete and I were at school we used to spend the summer holidays with an aunt of Dad's. It was quite near here, at Hengistbury.' Caryn sighed. 'Wonderful long summer days on the beach, swimming and scrambling up and down the cliffs.'

He smiled reminiscently. 'I know what you mean. I used to come and stay with Aunt Grace at Wessex House when I was a kid. Mike's family had a boat moored at Hengistbury, and I used to sail with them. Funny to think that we might even have met.'

'Oh, I doubt it. Aunt Jenny lived in a two-up-two-down fisherman's cottage, not a manor house,' said Caryn. 'We had to come here because we had no mother, and Dad couldn't cope with us in the holidays. I don't suppose *you* would have been allowed to play with the likes of us.'

Adam looked down at her, his eyes narrowing. 'I do hope you're not a snob, Caryn.'

'*Me*—a snob?'

'The inverted kind. Some of your remarks point that way.'

'That's nonsense.' The music came to an end and she said, 'If you don't mind, I think I'd like to go home.'

'To Wessex House, you mean?'

'It *is* still my home—for the present,' she said with a thrust of her chin. 'And I can't think of anything else to call it. Do you mind?'

Adam slipped a hand under her elbow. 'Not at all. I thought just for a moment that you'd become resigned to giving up your tenancy.'

She picked up her bag and tossed him a defiant look. 'Quite the contrary. First thing tomorrow I mean to take advice on the matter.'

He gave an exaggerated sigh. 'Oh, dear, and here was I thinking you were beginning to see sense on the subject.' He chuckled maddeningly. 'I'll get the car while you collect your coat.'

As he walked out to the car park he was deep in thought. When he picked Caryn up earlier he had been fairly sure she was about to use her feminine wiles on him. Dressed to kill and almost fluttering her eyelashes, she'd made some flimsy excuse as to why her brother couldn't join them and seemed more than happy to be with him alone. Later she'd seemed to be going out of her way to impress him with her professionalism. Now the only thing he could be sure of was that she resented him. She obviously loved Wessex House and wanted to remain there. It was going to be harder getting her and her brother out of the place than he had envisaged.

When he had discovered that Aunt Grace had left it to him he had been surprised and delighted. It was perfect for what he had in mind. Of course, he would have to obtain planning permission for the extensions he had in mind. There was a lot of work ahead—architects to talk to, builders to engage. It would all take time. Giving the Deans till the end of summer hadn't been as generous as it sounded. They were paying rent, after all. Might as well let them continue. On the other hand, the longer he let them stay, the harder it would be to get them out.

Nevertheless, as he slid on to the driving seat of the Porsche he was considering the possibility of extending the deadline. Caryn Dean was an intriguing girl. He'd never met anyone quite like her before. Most of the girls he knew went out of their way to please him. And Caryn had every reason to try to get on the right side of him. He found himself wanting to break through that prickly armour to the soft heart he suspected nestled inside. She was like a chestnut, he told himself, smiling at the metaphor, all spiky on the outside, crisply sweet inside.

Powdering her nose in the cloakroom, Caryn studied her reflection reproachfully.

'You'll blow everything if you're not careful, Caryn Dean,' she admonished. 'You and your quick tongue! If you let Pete down I'll never speak to you again. Better get out there and try to build a few bridges.'

As she came out through the swing doors Adam drew the car up to the steps. She slipped into the passenger-seat without a word and fastened her seatbelt.

'All right?' he looked enquiringly at her.

'Fine, thanks.' She glanced at him. 'Look, I'm sorry if I seem a bit hostile—Adam.'

'That's perfectly all right. I understand.'

'Do you?' she sighed. 'Wessex House is so important to me—and to Peter. I wonder if you can imagine what a shock it was to discover that it was to be taken away from us just as we're getting settled.'

'Of course I appreciate that,' Adam agreed.

She sighed. 'I'd do anything to stay there.'

He glanced at her, his eyebrows rising slightly. Did she mean what he thought she meant? Had he read her all wrong after all? He said nothing. Better to let her confirm or deny his suspicions herself.

'I might have known our luck wouldn't last,' she went on. 'Mike—Dr Faber has been so kind.'

'And now I've come along like the big bad wolf to ruin your dreams. Is that it?'

'Oh, no. I hope you don't think. . . I mean, it's your house. You have a perfect right to do as you wish with it.'

'Precisely.' Adam found himself wondering just what the relationship between Mike and Caryn was. Mike was a good sort; he wouldn't want to spoil things for him. And yet she seemed to be flashing all the signals. He pulled the car into a quiet lane and switched off the engine.

'When you say you'd do anything to stay at Wessex House, what did you have in mind?' His voice was warm and husky as he slid an arm along the back of the seat.

'Well—I thought more rent, perhaps?' she offered, glancing uneasily at the hand that appeared close to her ear. 'We couldn't afford much more, but if it would help. . .' She broke off as the hand moved to cup her shoulder, drawing her towards him. As he chuckled softly against her cheek his breath tickled her ear.

'Now, you know it isn't a question of money,' he said softly. 'That isn't what you meant at all, Caryn, is it?'

She shook her head. 'Now wait a minute. It was just—just a figure of speech. I——' Before she could continue his mouth covered hers, kissing her very firmly. With an indignant squeak she struggled free, and before he had time to say anything her hand lashed out, striking his cheek with a loud smack.

'Ow!' His astonished eyes stared down at her as he rubbed his stinging cheek. 'Was that necessary?'

'I might have asked *you* the same question. Just what do you take me for, *Mr* Laine?' He could see the almond-shaped eyes gleaming greenly at him through the dim light. She looked like an enraged tigress.

'It was only a harmless kiss, for heaven's sake,' he protested.

'I see—only a harmless kiss. If you wanted me to *pay* for my dinner you should have said.'

'It wasn't a question of that. I thought you wanted——'

'Wanted you to *kiss* me?' Caryn's eyes flashed fire at him. 'You've *got* to be joking. Let me tell you, Mr Laine, that I wouldn't want to kiss you if you were made of ice-cream. If I wanted you to kiss me I'd leave you in no doubt. . .' She broke off, aware that she was letting her tongue run away with her again.

'Well, maybe that's something to look forward to.' He tried hard not to smile. 'I'm sorry, Caryn, we've had our wires crossed. I think I'd better take you home before we make any more mistakes about each other.'

'Yes, I think that would be best,' she agreed.

They drove the rest of the way in silence, Caryn bristling with indignation in her seat, while Adam smiled to himself with maddening calm as he negotiated the powerful car through the twisting Dorset lanes.

Drawing the car to a standstill at the front door, he leaned across her to open the passenger door, but as he released the door catch he felt her stiffen.

'Don't worry, Caryn, I'm not looking for another slap. I'll be in touch again soon.'

'There's no hurry,' she said pointedly as she stepped out of the car on to the drve. 'But if you're really interested in our work, perhaps you'd like to attend one of our group therapy sessions. Who knows? You might learn a few things about yourself.'

Adam revved the engine angrily. '*No, thanks*!' he shouted above the noise. 'I leave that kind of thing to the self-indulgent!' He let out the clutch and turned the wheel sharply. Then, with a spinning of wheels that forced her to jump clear of flying gravel, he roared furiously away down the drive.

Fred Hastings usually arrived at Wessex House on Friday afternoons and stayed until Sunday evenings. He was a small, rotund man of fifty-five with a jolly round face and sensitive brown eyes. The female clients at Wessex House loved him. To many he was the 'father' they had never had, and Caryn found him invaluable in her group therapy sessions. He came whenever he could, arriving unannounced and without ceremony. If there wasn't a room for him he would cheerfully and uncomplainingly sleep on the chesterfield in the living-room at the lodge, and he was always willing to do anything from the most menial chore to sitting in on groups—something at which he was becoming more useful week by week.

Fred was a Yorkshireman. He had once been a master chef at one of the best hotels in the city of York. At thirty-five his life had been idyllic and full of promise. His career was assured, he had a pretty wife and an adorable little daughter. Then, overnight, disaster had struck. Katy, his wife, had been taken ill with viral pneumonia and died within days. His mother-in-law had taken the baby because Fred's working hours meant he could not care for her himself. Going home to an empty house, sometimes late at night, was sheer torture. Fred began to drink, at first to forget his unhappiness, then for comfort and to help him sleep, later to assuage the voracious habit that refused to release him.

Gradually his intake of alcohol affected his concentration and his memory, which cost him his job. Then one day the ultimate happened. It was on one of the precious days that he was in charge of his baby daughter. He left the child outside a shop in her pram and went home without her.

There was a hue and cry and the child was found, safe and well. But after that his mother-in-law refused him access to his daughter. His tragedy was complete. He had lost everything—his wife, his job, his baby daughter, and finally his self-respect. He sought the help of Lisa Gregory and tried his best to pull himself out of the helpless state he was in. It was a long haul, but eventually it paid off. Now that he was cured he gave all his spare time in trying to help others as he had been helped.

That Friday afternoon Caryn was more pleased than usual to see his stocky figure walking up the drive. Getting up from the desk that she and Peter shared in the office, she threw open the door as he stepped into the hall.

'Fred—how lovely to see you!'

The little man flushed with pleasure. 'Well, it's nice to get a welcome, love, but I was here last week. Anyone'd think you hadn't seen me for months.'

'A lot can happen in a week, Fred,' Caryn said. 'But come and have some tea and I'll tell you all about it.'

'Is Annie coming?' Fred asked later as they sat over tea.

Annie Thurston was another of the Wessex House regulars. She had been an anorexic and was one of Lisa Gregory's outstanding successes. She ran a craft centre quite near to Fortunes Cove, and as well as spending all of her out-of-season weekends at Wessex House she was always at the end of the telephone for help and advice in emergencies.

'Annie's already here,' Caryn told him with a smile. 'I don't know what we'd do without our willing helpers.'

'A chance to pay back a debt, that's what it is,' Fred

said, reaching for another biscuit. 'A lot of us wouldn't even be here today if it wasn't for folks such as you.'

'And *we* might not be here much longer,' Caryn said with a sigh. 'That's the news I told you about.'

Fred stopped, his cup halfway to his mouth as he stared at her. 'Not here—why? What's happened?'

'Wessex House has a new owner,' she told him. 'Old Mrs Laine died—well, you knew that. What you didn't know was that she left the house to her other nephew.'

'What—not Dr Faber?'

'That's right. Mr Adam Laine, her brother's son. He's a surgeon at a London hospital and a private clinic. He wants the house for his well-off patients to use as a convalescent home.'

Fred's eyes were round with dismay. 'No kidding? How long've you got?'

Caryn sighed. 'Till the end of the summer. I hoped we could fight it, but it seems we haven't a leg to stand on. To begin with, we rent the place furnished, which means we can be asked to leave at any time.'

'Have you taken legal advice?'

She nodded. 'There's nothing we can do. Our arrangement with Dr Faber was only verbal. He wasn't to know he wouldn't be our landlord for long. It isn't his fault.'

'What's he like—this surgeon?' asked Fred.

Caryn pulled a face. 'Awful—a sort of playboy type. His aunt obviously spoilt him rotten and he thinks the world is his oyster.'

Fred shrugged. 'Sounds like he's not far wrong at that.'

'Still, never mind,' Caryn said determinedly. 'We'll carry on our work if we have to hire a field to do it in.'

'That's the spirit,' Fred grinned. 'And you won't be alone, love. Not while I've got breath in my body. I dare say Annie's with me on that too. Now, who've we got with us this weekend?'

'The same crowd as last weekend,' she told him. 'Plus a new girl, Fleur Mason. She's anorexic. I'm a bit worried about her.'

From experience Caryn knew that anorexics often didn't respond well to group therapy. Bulimics and compulsive eaters were aware that they needed help, while anorexics invariably denied that they needed anyone or anything, which made them very hard to reach. However, Caryn urged them to sit in, in the hope that the communication of others might touch some chord. Even if they believed they needed nothing they might still be persuaded to *give* something—and in that way begin the long, slow business of returning to normal communication. In Fleur Mason's case she had so far come up against a brick wall. Since her arrival two days ago the girl had sat alone in her room. Her hospital treatment had ensured that her weight was back to a safe level and she was eating, albeit very little. But Caryn's subtle attempts to draw her out had so far met with stonewall silence. Invited to join the group that afternoon, she had simply shrugged and turned her face to the wall. Caryn doubted very much whether she would attend, and she had made up her mind that if she failed to turn up this time she would have to try a one-to-one approach.

In the pleasant garden-room at the back of the house a semi-circle of comfortable chairs was arranged. Clients were told that the session would start and end at given times and that they must be punctual. Discipline was something that was lacking in the lives of many of them. It was something they needed, and this responsibility to their therapist and to each other was a first and important step.

Four clients assembled that Friday afternoon, with
Fred and Annie sitting in and Caryn as therapist. When
the time came to begin and Fleur had not put in an
appearance Caryn took Annie to one side.

'Will you stand in and tape the session for me?' she
asked. 'I'd like to take Fleur myself. She's been here
two days and so far I haven't been able to get through
to her at all.'

She left them settling down and climbed the stairs to
Fleur's room. Tapping lightly on the door, she called,
'Fleur, can I come in?'

There was a murmur of assent from inside the room,
and Caryn opened the door to find the girl in her usual
position, in a chair near the window. She wore a pretty
flowered houscoat, but even the frilled collar and long
skirt failed to diguise her sadly emaciated body.

'I'm sorry about the group thing,' she said, glancing
at Caryn.

'That's all right. Look, I thought it might be nice if
we had a chat. I tell you what, I'm dying for a coffee.
Would you mind if I made one up here?'

Again the girl shrugged apathetically. 'Whatever you
like.'

Caryn filled the kettle and plugged it in. 'You'll have
one too, won't you?'

As she had expected, Fleur took her coffee black
and sugarless. She held the cup in both hands and
stared into it, her long fair hair hanging down on either
side of her face like curtains. It was as though she were
deliberately forming a barrier between herself and
Caryn.

'Fleur, you came here of your own free will, didn't
you?' Caryn asked gently. 'That must mean that you
want to get better.'

The girl gave a brittle little laugh. 'It's stupid. There's
nothing wrong with me—just because I don't want to

stuff myself with food all day long. People eat far too much.'

'You don't have to pretend with me, Fleur. Will you at least talk to me?'

'If I must,' shrugged Fleur. 'What do you want to know?'

'I want to know what you want to tell me.'

The girl looked up. 'The reason why I won't gorge myself and get fat, you mean? Why is everyone so obsessed with my eating habits?'

'I don't think they are.' Caryn got up and began to walk round the room. It was noticeable that there were few personal objects—no family photographs, no trinkets, perfume or make-up. But there was a small and much worn teddy-bear on the bed, half hidden under the duvet. She picked it up.

'You've had him a long time. He's only got one eye. What's his name?' she asked.

A slight flush coloured Fleur's cheek. 'He doesn't have one.'

'I had one just like this,' Caryn said. 'He's still around somewhere. There was a time when I used to tell him all my troubles. He always made them better.' She sat down again opposite Fleur, the bear in her lap. 'Tell me about home and your family. Your mother seems very nice. She's very beautiful, isn't she?'

'She runs a model agency,' Fleur said. 'She was a top model herself when she was younger.'

'That must make you very proud of her.'

Suddenly the girl's head came up and the vivid blue eyes met Caryn's. '*Proud*? You don't know what you're talking about,' she said bitterly. 'Her career spoilt everything. She never had time for Daddy and me. Daddy left in the end. I was six then. I wanted to go with him, but she packed me off to boarding-school instead. I never could do anything right for her, and

then when I left without any A levels she made me
start modelling.'

'You make it sound like a punishment. A lot of girls
would give their eye teeth for a modelling career,'
Caryn told her.

'But I was no good at it, and she should have known
I wouldn't be. I was fat and clumsy,' Fleur said
vehemently. 'Anyone could have seen that, for God's
sake. Anyone except my mother. I hated it. I wanted
to go to college and take art and design, but she
wouldn't let me.'

There was a pause, and Caryn noticed that the girl
was shaking. She reached out a hand to touch her, but
Fleur jerked her hand out of reach.

'Then she met Pierre,' she said quietly.

'Is that your stepfather?' Caryn remembered the
dark, good-looking man sitting in the car on the day
that Fleur had arrived. He had looked all of twenty
years younger than the girl's mother.

Fleur laughed drily. 'God forbid. He moved in a year
ago. He hates me—I'm in the way. It was his idea to
send me here.'

'Surely not?' queried Caryn.

'Yes, it was.' The blue eyes flashed fire. 'What do
you know about it?'

After a pause Caryn asked. 'Fleur, if you could
choose, if a fairy promised to grant you one wish, what
would it be?'

Fleur shrugged. 'I don't want anything. I don't *need*
anything.'

'I see.' Caryn sat for a moment, stroking the almost
bald teddy bear. 'I'll bet if he could talk he'd tell me,'
she said at last. 'He's known you all your life. There
can't be many things he doesn't know about you.'

The ghost of a smile twitched the corners of Fleur's
mouth.

'What do you think he'd choose for *his* one wish?' Caryn asked.

'To go back to when—when Daddy was there,' said Fleur without hesitation. For a moment the cornflower blue eyes were wistful, then she looked at Caryn and they clouded over again. 'Well, he had all his fur then, didn't he—and both eyes?'

'And what about you? What did you have?'

Fleur looked up, and just for a moment Caryn thought she was about to unburden herself, and then the shutters came down again and the girl leaned forward, letting her hair fall across her face again. 'I'm tired,' she said wearily. 'I'd like to go to sleep. Will you go now, please?'

CHAPTER THREE

'OH, NO, they're sniping at each other again. Are you sure these group therapy sessions are a good idea?'

Peter and Caryn were sitting in the office after dinner the following Monday evening, listening to the tape Caryn had made of the group therapy session that afternoon. Caryn switched off the tape recorder and turned to her brother.

'Their sniping at each other is very useful,' she told him. 'It helps get rid of their aggression, and it tells us a lot about them that we wouldn't hear otherwise. I'm sure it helped over the weekend, having Annie and Fred here. Having been through the mill themselves, they know how to draw the others out.'

Peter sighed. 'Give me the admin side every time,' he said. 'Just listening to it makes me tired.'

'Are you all right, Pete?' She looked at him with concern. 'Not in pain, are you?'

He shook his head. 'No more than usual. It's the uncertainty about Wessex House that's getting to me, if I'm honest.' He turned his chair towards her. 'By the way, you never actually told me how you got on with Adam Laine the other evening.'

To hide her sudden flush Caryn turned to take the tape out of the machine. 'I'm afraid it wasn't exactly what you'd call a roaring success,' she confessed. 'It looks as though we're definitely going to have to start looking for somewhere else.'

'Are you saying you didn't hit it off?'

'Exactly that.'

He sighed. 'Oh, really, Caryn, you might have made

an effort to be nice to him. You said yourself you'd hate to leave here.'

'Look, it was clear from the beginning that he's hell-bent on kicking us out. Anyway, he's awful.'

'In what way?' Peter's eyes narrowed.

'Just—*awful*, that's all.' Caryn picked up the tray with their after-dinner coffee-cups and headed for the door, but Peter wheeled his chair neatly between it and her.

'No, you don't. Just you sit down a minute and tell me about it. It's my future we're talking about as well as yours, you know.'

With a resigned sigh Caryn put the tray back on the desk and sat down. 'He must have got the wrong impression,' she said.

'Meaning?'

'It was probably my fault—something to do with the way I dressed—something I said.'

'Exactly *what* was your fault?'

She shrugged.

'Caryn,' Peter looked exasperated, 'are you going to tell me what happened?'

'Oh, he—made a pass and I. . .' Caryn winced and bit her lip. 'I hit him.'

'*Bloody hell*!' Peter clapped one hand to his forehead and stared at her. 'You don't do things by halves, do you? So how did it end up?'

'How do you mean—end up?'

'How did you part, of course? Friends or enemies?'

Caryn swallowed hard. 'Well, shall we say not quite what you'd call the best of friends?'

'I don't believe I'm hearing this,' groaned Peter. 'You should have let *me* go out to dinner with him.'

'The thing is, what happens next?' she asked.

'Why ask me?' he looked at her. 'But since you have, I'll tell you what happens next. You *apologise*.'

'I *what*?' she echoed.

'You heard me. You tell him you're sorry. You tell him as quickly as possible. And you make him believe that you *mean* it.'

Caryn jumped to her feet. 'You've got to be joking.'

'Not a chance. Do it, Caryn. Ring Mike and ask when his cousin will be down again. Make an appointment to see him.' Peter reached for the telephone. 'In fact, I'll do it myself—now.' He dialled the number and looked up at his sister's red face as he waited for a reply. 'I'm serious about this, Caryn. This is no game we're playing. We can't afford a battle of the sexes. Where do you thing I'm going to get a job in my state of——' He broke off as Mike lifted the receiver at the other end.

'Oh, Mike. Hi. Peter here. We—Caryn and I wondered when Adam would be down again. We'd like to arrange. . .' he glanced up at Caryn, who pulled a face at him '. . . a meeting. There are things to discuss.'

Caryn waited, trying in vain to hear what Mike was saying at the other end. Peter's face cleared.

'This weekend? Oh, good. Maybe he'd like to come to dinner. You too, of course, Mike. You'll ring me back and let me know? Great. Bye, then.' He replaced the receiver and looked at Caryn. 'You'd better make a trip into town tomorrow and get something special for dinner,' he told her grimly.

Her eyes opened wide. 'If you think *I'm* cooking dinner—waiting on that—that. . .'

'That *landlord*?' Peter supplied. 'The one we're trying so hard to impress and keep on the right side of?'

'There are limits,' she protested.

He shook his head at her. 'I could have said that to you.' His expression softened. 'Caryn—look, love, beggars can't be choosers. I accept that you probably hate the guy's guts, but right at this moment we simply can't afford to take a high-handed attitude.' His lips twitched in the ghost of a grin. 'And you did say it was probably your fault. By the way, what *did* you wear?'

'The black velvet ski pants and the jacket.'

'The one with all the colours? Pheeew.' He gave a long, low whistle. 'In that case, you only got what you deserved.'

'Don't be so sexist. I just wanted to look nice for a change. I get fed up with jeans and T-shirts.'

'Yes, but as you said, there *are* limits. That outfit might be OK for a London nightclub, but down here. . .' He broke off to chuckle. 'I must say I'd like to have been a fly on the wall. I remember how hard you can thump from when we were kids.'

'It wasn't funny,'

'No? Well, never mind, you're going to get the chance to put things right, aren't you?' Peter wheeled himself to the door and opened it. 'I think I'll go down to the lodge now and have an early night. I dare say you'd like some time to yourself—to plan the menu for our little dinner party.'

Caryn threw the first thing that came to hand, which was the telephone pad. It struck the wall and fell harmlessly to the floor as Peter pulled the door closed behind him.

When Mike still hadn't rung back next morning Caryn's hopes began to rise. Perhaps Adam wasn't coming down for the weekend after all. Perhaps she was going to get out of the dreaded dinner and apology. But it was as she was talking to Maggie after breakfast about the day's menus that Mike arrived. He'd come to give Fleur her medical. She was the centre's newest client, and it was part of the policy of Gregory centres to have a doctor examine new clients as soon as possible after checking in.

'I thought I'd kill two birds with one stone,' he said as he followed Caryn up the stairs. 'I was called out last night just after Peter rang.'

'I see.' She glanced at him. 'So you didn't get a chance to speak to Adam?'

'Oh, yes. I rang him, but it was too late to ring you back then.' He smiled. 'We'd love to come to dinner. Adam was really pleased when I told him.' He smiled. 'And as it looks as though it'll be the only chance I shall have of seeing you I'm pleased too.'

Caryn avoided his eyes. 'Sorry, Mike, but life's been a bit hectic lately.'

'I know. Would Saturday be convenient?'

Her heart sank at the prospect of the dinner party. She had pinned all her hopes on Adam's wanting to keep his distance after their last disastrous meeting. Clearly he was looking forward to watching her grovel. But in spite of her dismay she managed to force some enthusiasm into her voice.

'Oh—yes, Saturday would be fine.' They had reached the landing and she tapped on Fleur's door. 'Fleur, may I come in? The doctor's here to see you.'

They found the girl up and dressed. When Caryn introduced Mike the girl stared resentfully at him. 'I thought I'd left doctors behind at the hospital,' she said bluntly.

He gave her his goodnatured grin as he put his bag down on the dressing-table. 'I know, it's not fair, is it, Fleur?' he said. 'But don't worry, this is just the routine check we have to do when you arrive. After this you won't see me again unless you ask for me.'

'Well, I shan't do that.' In spite of her obvious resentment, the girl relaxed slightly and submitted herself to Mike's routine examination. 'Aren't you going to ask me what I'm eating?' she challenged as she rolled down her sleeve after having her blood-pressure taken.

Mike put away his sphygmomanometer and looked up. 'Not unless you particularly want to tell me about it,' he said mildly. He looked at Caryn. 'That reminds me—I suppose you've cleared away breakfast?'

She smiled. 'Yes, but I dare say we can find you a cup of coffee and some fresh toast.'

He stood up and smiled warmly at Fleur. 'See how well they look after you here? That's fine, Fleur. Sorry to intrude on you so early in the morning. I know you'll like it here at Wessex House. Just let Caryn know if you ever need to see me.'

Fleur gave him the ghost of a smile and turned towards her chair by the window.

On the landing Caryn looked at him. 'Everything all right?' she asked.

He sighed. 'Underweight, of course, but that's to be expected. Is she eating?'

'They got her eating again a little while she was in hospital. She wasn't allowed to leave until her weight was up and her menstrual cycle had resumed. I talked to her a little yesterday. She's a classic case, and unfortunately we know from experience that they almost always slide back after hospitalisation. Now if I can only get her mixing with the others a little—get her into group therapy. . .'

'It's a very specialised field,' said Mike. 'Very complex. I really admire the work you're doing here. We GPs don't have nearly enough time to give to cases like this.' He smiled. 'But you know where I am if you need me.' He glanced at his watch. 'Now, did you mention coffee and toast? I think I've just got time.'

Maggie had already put a tray in the office. When he

saw it Mike beamed. 'Maggie Cookson's a real treasure.'

'I couldn't agree with you more, and we have you to thank for recommending her,' Caryn said as she poured two cups.

He sipped his coffee gratefully. 'I know she was grateful for a job where she could work flexible hours. She never quite knows how Jim will be from one day to the next.'

'She thinks the world of you for all you did for him,' said Caryn.

'No more than for any other patient. MS can be managed with care and patience, once the patient has learned to accept it. He and Maggie co-operate. You'd be surprised how many don't.'

Caryn laughed. 'No, I wouldn't, especially not in this job.'

Mike looked round. 'No Peter this morning?'

'It's his morning for physio. He left for the hospital right after breakfast.' She paused. 'I wanted to have a word with you about him, Mike. He's been having quite a bit of pain lately. He doesn't say anything, of course, but I can always tell.'

Mike sighed. 'That's the trouble with partial paralysis. The damaged nerves are causing the problem. I'm hoping it'll improve. The physio should help.'

She looked at him. 'The uncertainty about our future isn't helping either. I expect you know that we're under notice to leave here?'

He sighed. 'Adam did tell me a little about his plans. He's cagey about them, though. I dare say he doesn't want to count his chickens.'

'It's not fair, Mike,' she burst out. 'Surely we have *some* rights?'

'I'm afraid not, love, and I blame myself. If only I'd been a better businessman and had a proper legal contract drawn up, things would have been a great deal more secure for you.'

'Oh, no, Mike, it isn't your fault and we're not blaming you at all.' She sighed. 'I just can't understand how you and he can be related and yet be so different.'

'You do at least have until the end of the summer, though.'

She sighed. 'Well, I hope so. I'm afraid he might change his mind about that, though.'

He gave her a sidelong glance. 'Am I to take it that you and he didn't hit it off when you went out to dinner?'

Caryn looked up in time to catch his wistful expression. 'We just don't understand each other, Mike. We don't speak the same language, and I don't think we ever could in a thousand years—even if either of us wanted to,' she added conclusively.

He grinned. 'Oh, dear, that sounds pretty final. But maybe when you know him better. . . He probably isn't as bad as you think, Caryn. Adam never had a proper family life as I did as a kid. His mother was a beautiful woman who never settled to being a doctor's wife. She ran away with an American actor when Adam was six. After that his father seemed to lose all interest in life, his young son included. Adam was sent away to school and in the holidays he came here to Aunt Grace. She was the only mother he ever really knew.'

'Which is why she left him the house.'

'Exactly. She was always aware of the fact that she fell far short of a small boy's expectations of a mother. For that reason she always felt he needed some kind of anchor—stability in his adult life.'

Caryn shrugged. In her opinion Adam was just a 'poor little rich boy' who had grown up into a self-centred man. She and Peter had lost their mother too. They had had to be farmed out with an aunt in the holidays, but it hadn't made them hard, uncaring and avaricious.

'For all his traumatic childhood he seems stable enough to me,' she said pointedly.

'Ah, but none of us can ever really know what goes on in the mind of another, can we?'

Caryn said nothing. She felt she knew *more* than enough about the workings of Adam Laine's mind. But Peter had been right; if only for his sake she was going to have to swallow her pride and try and make herself agreeable to their new landlord, and she wasn't looking forward to it. Not one little bit.

Mike stood up. 'Well, I dare say you have your work to attend to, and I'm due in surgery in ten minutes.' He bent to kiss her cheek. 'We'll see you on Saturday evening, then. I take it that will be at the lodge?'

She nodded. 'About eight for half-past. Peter and I are looking forward to it,' she lied.

In the lounge the clients were gathered. Annie had some time off and had stayed on after the weekend to help. When Caryn came in she was talking to Sarah, a young bulimic mother. Sarah was twenty-eight and had two delightful young sons and an adoring husband. She ran a successful domestic agency and had managed successfully to hide her bulimia from those close to her for years. When her husband had come home one day to find her vomiting violently in the bathroom he had thought she was ill. When he had discovered that it was a daily occurrence he had been shocked and begged her to have treatment.

She had been at Wessex House for a week, but so far Caryn had not been able to gain any insight into the cause of her trouble.

Unlike Fleur, Sarah was bright and outgoing. She had a pleasant personality, and outwardly it was

impossible to guess that anything troubled her at all.
She was also trying very hard to overcome what was
now an irresistible urge to binge on food in private and
later disgorge it. But denying herself the one thing that
she felt she needed wasn't going to effect a permanent
cure, as Caryn knew.

She smiled at Annie and took her aside. 'I'd be
grateful if you'd go up and try to talk to Fleur,' she
said. 'Tell her about your own experience. See if you
can persuade her to come down and join the others.
We have the occupational therapist coming this afternoon. Fleur mentioned yesterday that she wanted to
study art. Maybe Jilly could get her started.'

Annie nodded. 'I'll see what I can do.'

When she had gone Caryn sat down beside Sarah,
who was knitting. 'Is that for one of your boys?' she
asked.

The girl looked up. She had large and beautiful
brown eyes that were always ready with a smile, but at
close quarters Caryn thought she saw pain and something close to fear lurking in their liquid depths.

'It's for John.' She held up the small Aran sweater.
'He's growing so fast—they both are.'

'Tell me about them.' Caryn listened as the woman
enthused about her two sons. She obviously loved and
missed them both very much.

'You know, you don't have to stay here for long
periods,' Caryn told her. 'You live quite near, so you
can come for the odd day if you like. Fit it in with your
business.'

Sarah put down her knitting and looked at Caryn.
'It's so peaceful and relaxed here,' she said. 'No one
fires questions at you or makes you feel like a freak.
No one expects anything of you. You make us feel we
count.'

'I'm sure you count to your family,' said Caryn, instantly picking up on the word.

Sarah's eyes clouded. 'Oh, yes, I do.'

'And to your clients and employees.'

'Yes.'

'But you don't count to yourself—is that what you feel?' Caryn asked gently.

Sarah's eyes widened slightly. 'How did you know?'

'It's my job,' Caryn smiled. 'While you're here I want you to think about that, Sarah. Ask yourself why you feel so badly about yourself. If you want to—and *only* if you want to, you can talk to me about it.' She stood up. 'In the meantime just relax. Sometimes we have lovely walks on the cliffs or by the sea, I hope you'll join us.'

'Oh, I will.'

As Caryn turned away she reflected that in her own way Sarah, for all her 'sweet reasonableness', was as difficult to help as the silent, reclusive Fleur.

On Saturday evening Caryn had the table laid in plenty of time. She had chosen her best lace cloth and arranged spring flowers in a posy round the single yellow candle in the centre. She had taken special care over the meal too. A light, clear soup to start with, chicken in a tangy orange sauce, with fresh spring vegetables and tiny new potatoes, and, for dessert, a raspberry cheesecake, made herself the previous evening. Now the only remaining problem was what to wear. Peter had already asked what she had in mind, an anxious expression on his face.

'How about a fetching little number in sackcloth and ashes?' she'd asked facetiously. 'Don't worry, I'm planning to look like Goody Two-Shoes. I don't want to fight off another of his passes.'

'You should be so lucky,' Peter had told her.

'*Lucky*?' she echoed.

'Well, hooking the rich owner of the house wouldn't be such a bad move, would it?'

Caryn gave an explosive snort. 'Marry that insufferable swine?'

'You're over-reacting again. Anyway, you won't get the chance now. Blown it good and proper, haven't you?' He knew he was pushing his luck and warded off Caryn's withering look with a mischievous grin.

In her room Caryn took out a well-cut black skirt and a blouse in lemon chiffon with a high frilled neck and tiny pintucks. She arranged her hair as neatly as its springy nature would allow and applied a very subtle make-up. When she was ready she gave her reflection a long look. That ought to be demure enough, even for Peter, she told herself. Until now she had deliberately shut the apology she was to make out of her mind. When should she deliver it? The idea of Peter and Mike witnessing her humiliation was unthinkable. But if she engineered a situation where she was left alone with Adam, would he misinterpret her motives?

'Yes, he would,' she said aloud. 'He's obviously accustomed to having females chasing him.' She screwed up her face into a fierce grimace, wishing the coming evening were over and behind her.

Once dressed and ready, she went into the kitchen to put the finishing touches to the meal, and it was there that Mike found her five minutes later, decorating the cheesecake with swirls of whipped cream.

'Mmm, that looks good enough to eat.'

She looked up in surprise. 'Mike, you're early.' She tugged at the strings of her apron. 'Where's—er. . .?'

He smiled. 'Don't panic. Adam had to slip into Dorchester this afternoon to see Aunt Grace's solicitor again, so I came on ahead. I need my own car anyway, in case I get called out.'

'He went to the solicitors?' Caryn asked, frowning. 'On a Saturday afternoon?'

Mike nodded. 'He'd mislaid some important document or other last time Adam was over. He rang him yesterday to say he'd found it and he wanted Adam to see it as soon as possible.'

'I see.' Cary slid the decorated dessert carefully back into the fridge. 'Well, so long as you're early how about a sherry?'

'Sounds lovely.' He watched as she poured a drink, reflecting that she seemed to grow lovelier every time he saw her. As he took the glass from her she caught his look.

'Mike? What is it? You've come early on purpose, haven't you?'

'Oh dear, am I as transparent as that?' He took a sip of his sherry, then went on, 'I never was much of a hand at subtlety, and maybe this isn't the ideal time. But lately it's been well nigh impossible to see you alone.'

'Is something wrong, Mike?' she asked anxiously. 'You want to warn me about something, is that it?'

'No, nothing like that.' He tossed back the remainder of his drink and took a deep breath. 'Look, it's this. There's a way out of your problem.'

'There is?' Her face brightened hopefully.

'Yes. If you agree, that is.'

She waited, but Mike simply cleared his throat and slipped one finger round the inside of his collar.

'Well, are you going to tell me what it is?'

'It's simple really. Why don't you just—just marry me?'

There was a stunned silence as they stared at each other, then Caryn said, 'Oh, Mike. . .'

He held up his hand. 'No, don't say anything until you've had time to think about it. You see, I was thinking—I have plenty of room. We could turn half the ground floor into a treatment centre. . .'

'But—Peter,' she reminded him.

He stopped and looked at her. 'What do you mean—Peter?'

'Peter has to have a home too—and a job.'

'There'd be room for him too. And I could always find him plenty of paperwork.'

She shook her head. 'He'd see that as charity. He'd never agree.'

'But you have your life too, Caryn. The important thing is, what do *you* feel? Would you marry me—aside from the other problems, because if the answer is yes. . .'

'It *isn't*.' Too late she saw the hurt expression on his face and added, 'Oh, Mike, I'm sorry, I didn't mean to sound so brutal. It's just that I don't want you to start planning. You see, I don't want to marry anyone—not at the moment.'

'I understand. You're still in love with Richard, aren't you?'

She shook her head. 'No, not any more. When Peter had his accident our lives changed. It was painful at the time, but now I realise that I'm a changed person. I have to settle down a lot more, Mike, get to know this new person I've become before I start thinking about any new relationships.'

His face brightened. 'You mean there's a chance you might consider it—later?'

'I don't know. I honestly can't see it happening, Mike. I have to be honest with you. But I want you to know how much I appreciate your asking me.' She went to him and stood on tiptoe to kiss his cheek. His arms slid round her and held her for a moment as he said against her hair,

'I'd try to make you happy, Caryn. Since Claire died there's never been anyone else—till now.'

She felt her heart twist inside her. If only she *could* fall in love with Mike. He deserved better than what she was handing him. And it would make everything so simple. 'I'm lucky to have a friend like you, Mike,' she whispered huskily. 'I'll always appreciate your friendship.' She forced a light laugh past the lump in her throat. 'Now, what about another sherry?'

At the moment that Mike was making his tentative proposal to Caryn, Adam Laine was driving towards Fortune Cove, his mind spinning furiously.

The document Grace Laine's solicitor had mislaid had turned out to be in the form of a letter, deposited with him by Mrs Laine some months before her death, with instructions that it should not be opened until after her demise. Godfrey Haversham had telephoned Adam in London to say that it had been found, and that when it was opened, it had been found to contain a codicil to the old lady's will. He refused to disclose its contents, but had indicated that it contained something important. He had suggested that Adam come to his home at his earliest possible convenience.

The elderly solicitor looked grave as they faced each other across the desk in the study of his home.

'The late Miss Laine's instructions as laid down in this codicil concern Wessex House,' he told Adam. 'I think perhaps it's best if you read it yourself.'

The old man passed the sheet of embossed blue notepaper over the desk, and Adam read silently. He had only read halfway down the page when he looked up, his eyes wide with dismay.

'But it says I may only inherit Wessex House if I live in it as a family—with my *wife and children*,' he said incredulously. 'She *knew* I had no plans to marry, so why on earth. . .?'

'I think your aunt was anxious that you should marry,' old Mr Haversham said mildly. 'She spoke of it to me many times. She felt you'd missed a normal family life with—your late father being—well—er. . .' He cleared his throat discreetly.

'With my father being an incurable drunk, you mean?' Adam stood up to pace the room angrily. '*Damn* it. Why do one's elderly relatives feel obliged to try to run one's life?' he muttered. 'I'm not in the least maladjusted, alcoholic father or no. I know exactly what I want to do with my life, and it doesn't include a wife and family. She *knew* that, so why did she have to go and mess it up completely for me?' He snatched up the letter angrily and looked at the date. 'You don't think she wrote this in a confused state of mind, do you?'

The solicitor gave an apologetic smile. 'I'm afraid not. I saw her myself on the day she brought it into the office. She took me out to lunch, and she was as clear-minded as you or me.' He shook his head. 'I must confess, she spoke of making this condition when we drew up her will. I advised against it, but it seems she chose to ignore my advice after all.'

Adam sighed impatiently. 'And to think it almost never came to light. It's a pity the damned thing didn't *remain* lost.' He looked up hopefully. 'There isn't a chance that it could be illegal, I suppose?'

'I'm afraid there's no chance of that either.' The old man pointed to the foot of the paper. 'That's what I mean when I say that she knew what she was doing. She's even had it witnessed. You have one year to move into Wessex House as a married man. If you fail to comply, the house is to be sold and the proceeds given to charity.'

Mr Haversham looked up at Adam over the tops of his rimless glasses. 'It seems you have just twelve months to find yourself a wife, Mr Laine. It's that or lose the house.'

Caryn sensed Adam's anger the moment she answered his ring at the bell, but she carefully arranged her features into a smile as she held out her hand in a welcoming gesture.

'Good evening—Adam. I'm so glad you were able to come.'

He looked slightly taken aback. 'Good evening. It's good of you to ask me.'

'Mike's already here. Do come in and have a drink.'

The four of them sat sipping sherry and making polite small talk until Caryn felt she would explode with the tension. Jumping up, she said brightly, 'Well, if everyone's ready I'll serve dinner now. I hope you're all hungry.'

The room looked pretty, lit by one softly shaded lamp and the gentle glow of the single yellow candle on the table. The meal Caryn had planned and cooked with such care was delicious, but the three men merely picked at their food while she shot anxious glances round the table.

Peter did his best to keep the conversation flowing, but it was clear to Caryn that he was having one of his spells of pain. Mike looked depressed, which made her feel guilty. But it was Adam's face that cast a cloud over the whole proceedings. He wore a look of sheer belligerence, which she felt was totally uncalled-for. From the moment they sat down at the table she could see that the evening was going to be a failure, and by the time they reached the coffee stage her face ached with the pain of keeping the smile nailed to it. She knew she must get her dreaded apology over and done with so that they could call it a day.

Piling the used coffee-cups on to a tray, she said, 'I'll just take these to the kitchen and then, if you don't mind, Adam, there's something I'd like to speak to you about.' She swallowed hard and shot Peter an appealing look. 'Perhaps you and Mike would like to relax with a brandy while I take Adam for a walk round the garden.'

He nodded encouragingly. 'Yes, of course.'

Caryn tried hard to keep up a flow of light chatter as they walked up the drive towards the house. Adam replied in monosyllables, until suddenly he turned to her and said:

'Look, let's forget the small talk, shall we? Just tell me.'

She stopped in mid-sentence, her mouth agape. 'Tell you—what?'

'Whatever it is we've come out here for. What is it—some roof slates off? Or loose paving slabs on the terrace?'

'Oh, I see what you mean.' She laughed nervously. 'Neither of those. Anyway, there wouldn't be much point now, would there?'

'Then what *is* it?' he demanded tetchily. 'Could you get to the point? It's none too warm out here, and I feel the need of a brandy too.'

'Oh, dear. Was the meal. . .' She'd been going to say 'that bad?' but she stopped herself just in time. That was likely to trigger another row, and she was supposed to be out here to apologise. She took a deep breath.

'Well, if you want to know, I brought you out here to say I'm sorry,' she said quickly. The words felt like barbed wire on her tongue and she felt hot colour burning her cheeks. After a moment's silence she stole a glance at him. He looked nonplussed.

'Sorry? For what?'

She ground her teeth. He really *did* intend to get his pound of flesh, didn't he? 'For slapping you the other night. I—I realise now that I must have given you the wrong impression.'

'Oh, *that*?' He looked amused. 'Right, apology accepted,' he said with a magnanimity that made her squirm. 'As a matter of interest, what impression *did* you intend to give?'

'None that I'm aware of,' she told him smartly. 'The clothes I wore were ones I haven't worn for some time. Not since I used to go nightclubbing with my fiancé. I should have realised that they're not suitable for a quiet Dorset backwater.'

'I thought you looked very fetching.'

'Thank you.'

They strolled on for a moment or two, then Adam said, 'I wasn't aware that you were engaged. You told me you had no romantic attachments.'

'I haven't. I should have said *ex*-fiancé. My engagement was broken off soon after Peter's accident.'

'Oh. By you or by him?'

Caryn stopped walking. 'Look—I've apologised, which is what I intended to do. We might as well go back to the lodge now. Then you can have that brandy.'

Adam smiled maddeningly. 'In other words: mind you own business, Adam Laine.' The smile left his face as he caught her expression. 'Now it's my turn to apologise,' he said quietly. 'I'm sorry, it was an insensitive question.'

'Not at all.' She began to quicken her pace as they retraced their steps.

'I think I already owed you an apology anyway,' he said, matching his pace to hers. 'I behaved like a boor all through your excellent dinner. My only excuse is that I've had a hell of a day.'

'I hardly noticed your boorishness. Please don't feel you have to——'

He grasped her arm and forced her to stop walking. 'Wait a minute.'

They stood staring at each other, each of them a little breathless. Adam said, 'Caryn, do you think we could stop sniping, wipe the slate and start again? You've apologised for slapping me. I've apologised for being an insensitive boor. Could we be friends now?'

'I suppose we should at least try, as you're going to be our landlord for the next five months,' she agreed.

He was about to tell her that he was unlikely to be her landlord for very much longer when suddenly he looked at her. Her cheeks were pink and her eyes were sparkling. She was looking up at him, her lips slightly parted. She had the softest mouth he had ever seen, and suddenly he found himself remembering the delicious feel of those lips on his.

It was then that an idea began to form in his mind; an idea so crazy and incredible that he thrust it aside immediately.

He took her arm firmly. 'Let's go in,' he said. 'I think we could both do with a brandy.'

CHAPTER FOUR

'YOU'RE getting very cagey, Caryn. You never told me how Adam Laine took your apology last week,' Peter said as he pored over the morning mail. 'Still, I must say he looked in a better mood when you got back from your walk.' He looked up at her across the desk that they shared. 'What did you say to him?'

'I apologised, that's all. And he accepted my apology graciously. That's all there is to tell.' Caryn looked up from a batch of junk mail she was busy tearing up. 'Where *does* all this stuff come from? Oh, and by the way, he apologised to me too. He said he'd been boorish during dinner that evening because he'd had a bad day.'

Peter laughed. 'Well, well, you *are* getting along well. Next thing we know the pair of you'll be getting married!'

'On the contrary, with a bit of luck we won't see too much of him now until the end of summer. Which reminds me, have we done anything yet about finding somewhere to move to?'

'Already done,' Peter said. 'I gave the estate agents a ring last week.' He waved a sheaf of leaflets at her. 'These just came this morning. All we have to do now is look them over and find the right one.'

'Let's hope it'll be as easy as you make it sound,' Caryn said, looking at her watch. 'Unfortunately I'll have to leave you to it now. Time for me to make a start.'

* * *

Just three women had assembled for group therapy that morning, and Caryn was pleased to see that Fleur was one of them. She looked pale and nervous, but at least she had dressed in a neat skirt and sweater and tied up her long fair hair in a ponytail. The girl's vulnerability struck Caryn strongly. She looked like her name, flower-like and ethereal, and Caryn longed to be able to help her. There had been a telephone call from Fleur's mother the previous day to say she intended to visit shortly, and Caryn had decided to speak to her about family therapy. After what she had learned about Fleur's background she felt sure they would benefit from it.

Sarah looked bright and cheerful as usual and had brought her knitting along. As far as Caryn kew she had not indulged in one of her 'binges' since she arrived at Wessex House. Neither had she shown any indication that she would speak to anyone about herself. Perhaps this morning something would happen to induce her to open up and give Caryn a few clues.

The other member of the group was Helen, who was a compulsive eater. She was a tall girl of nineteen, who would have been extremely attractive if it were not for her weight problem. Helen's medical notes indicated that she was prone to mood swings and could go from restless high spirits to deep depression in a matter of minutes, and for no apparent reason. But Caryn was of the opinion that it was the drugs Helen had been prescribed, rather than her condition, that was causing her mood swings.

She put the three women at their ease by chatting in a relaxed way for five minutes, easing gradually into the subject they were there to discuss.

'Although the three of you have different problems there's one thing you all have in common,' she said at last. 'And that's food. Perhaps you'd agree with that?'

'You can say that again,' sighed Helen. 'But as far as I'm concerned, it isn't for the want of trying. I wouldn't mind betting you I've tried every diet there is. I've even had surgery to stop me eating.'

Sarah looked up from her knitting with a flicker of interest. 'Surgery? An operation, do you mean?'

'I had my jaws wired together,' Helen explained with a hint of pride. 'It was agony. I could only take liquids. Couldn't speak, couldn't laugh, couldn't even clean my teeth.'

'It sounds awful. Did it work?' Sarah asked.

The other girl shook her head gloomily. 'The moment they took the wiring out I started stuffing again. I just couldn't help it. Only wish I could.' She leaned forward confidentially. 'Do you know, there was a woman at the hospital who told me she'd had a stomach bypass. *She* lost weight all right. Then she had to have plastic surgery to get rid of all the loose skin.'

Caryn could see Fleur turning pale green. Another moment and the girl would leave. She said quickly, 'Perhaps we should start by introducing ourselves. Would you each like to say a little about your background—family and so on?'

Before she could try to ease Fleur into the discussion Helen spoke up again. 'I don't have any family. I lived with a boyfriend for a while, but my appetite disgusted him and he left.'

'Did that affect your eating habits?' asked Caryn.

'Yes. He tried to help at first—used to monitor my diet. Then he found I was eating in secret and he got really fed up with me. When he first left it was lovely to be able to eat as much as I liked, *when* I liked, and not have to sneak off to the bathroom with packets of crisps stuffed up my jumper. But that didn't last.' Sudden tears welled up in Helen's eyes. 'I got a sort of delayed reaction. God, I missed him so *much* when the novelty wore off. That made me depressed, and I ate even more *because* I was depressed, and. . .' She lifted her hands in a helpless gesture. 'Well, look at me now.'

'Would you eat normally if you got him back?' asked Sarah.

Helen shrugged. 'That's the awful part—I honestly don't know. I wish I did.' She peered at Sarah. 'Anyway, what's your problem? You look great to me.'

Sarah shrugged noncomittally. 'It's much the same as yours, really.'

'No kidding?' Helen stared at her. 'You stuff like me, you mean? But you're so slim.'

Sarah shot a pleading look at Caryn, who said gently: 'It's OK to talk about your problems, Sarah. That's what you're here for. Just let go. There's no need to worry or feel guilty about it here.'

Sarah looked slightly reassured. 'Well, I do binge in secret,' she said. 'But I—make myself get rid of it again immediately afterwards, I feel so ashamed.' She flushed. 'Revolting, isn't it?'

'Oh, that's nothing to worry about. I do it too sometimes.' Helen moved along the settee to sit closer to Sarah. 'You and I should get together. Maybe we could be mates—help each other.' She put out her hand to touch the other girl's arm, but Sarah stiffened slightly and moved away.

Caryn looked at Fleur. 'We haven't heard anything from you yet, Fleur. Would you like to comment on anything that's been said?'

'Only that I think gluttony is utterly degrading,' the girl said with a look of distaste. 'I like to be in control, and it seems to me that eating like that is totally lacking in discipline.'

Helen raised her eyebrows. 'Oh, *dear*! Listen to Miss Holier-than-thou! If you call looking like something out of a concentration camp being *in control* you must be barmy. What's your problem, then—anorexia? You think that's a bit more upmarket, do you? Seems to me you ought to try and eat a bit more before you slip down the plughole.'

Fleur looked superior. 'That was the attitude of the nurses at the hospital—my mother too. Only they were kinder and less outspoken about it.' Two spots of bright colour burned her cheeks. 'They made me eat— stood over me until I did. They gave me little treats when I ate up my meals and took away my TV set when I didn't. They wanted me to look like *you*, you see—to be fat and ugly. They tried to take away all my *control*, and I hated them for it.'

'It sounds to me as though they were trying to be nice to you,' said Helen. 'I should be so lucky. No one's ever nice to me. No one wants to know a fat girl.'Her eyes filled with tears again. 'Look at me—I'm a mess. You should have heard what Liam, my boy-friend, called me on the day he left.'

Fleur's expression was a mixture of shame and disgust, and Caryn stepped in quickly before the situation could become too embarrassing. Moving across to sit between Sarah and Helen on the settee, she offered the weeping girl a tissue.

'Listen,' she said. 'I want to say something to you all. Whether you realise it or not, you three have taken a very important step by coming here to Wessex House. You've acknowledged that you have a problem, and by acknowledging it and seeking help you've taken the first positive step towards overcoming it.'

'Can you really cure us?' Helen asked, sniffing into her tissue.

'No. You're here to cure yourselves,' Caryn told her. 'I'm here to help you as much as I can. But I can't do anything unless you let me. I'm ready at any time to talk, when and where you like and for as long as you need me. And of course you can talk to each other. Remember, you aren't the only person in the world with a problem.'

It was on Thursday afternoon that the flowers arrived. A florist's van drew up outside Wessex House to deliver a huge sheaf of beribboned red roses. Maggie took them in and carried them through to the office, her eyes shining with excitement.

'You must have a secret admirer, Miss Dean. Aren't they just beautiful? There must be at least four dozen.'

Caryn smiled, burying her nose in the fragrant crimson blooms. 'I'm afraid it's nothing so romantic. There must be some mistake. Either that or they're for one of our clients.' She searched the fancy paper the flowers were wrapped in for a card and found one tied to the stems.

'Well, *are* they for you?' Peter asked, looking up from his desk. 'Don't you realise that Maggie and I are dying of suspense?'

Caryn pushed the card back inside the paper surrounding the bouquet and headed for the door, her cheeks pink. 'Yes, they are for me, as a matter of fact,' she said briefly. 'I'd better put them in water before they start to wilt. Excuse me.'

In the empty kitchen she unwrapped the flowers and laid them on the worktop. Then she looked again at the card, her eyes incredulous as she read its message again.

> *One who can apologise so prettily deserves a little reward. Hope to see you again at the weekend. Adam.*

Was he being sarcastic? Surely he wouldn't choose expensive out-of-season roses with which to show his contempt. So he was about to descend on them again this weekend, was he? In spite of herself she felt a little *frisson* of excitement run through her veins, and immediately despised herself for it. She was done with all that. How could she be so weak and stupid as to allow a bunch of flowers and a few soft words to manipulate her? If he did show up this weekend she would show him—politely, of course—that she was no push-over.

It was nine-thirty, and Caryn and Peter were tidying up in the office, prior to going home to the lodge, when Peter suddenly said,

'Do you like Jilly?'

Caryn looked up in surprise. 'Occupational therapist Jilly, you mean?'

'Of course. We don't know any other Jilly, do we?'

She looked up quickly at his sharp tone. 'Of course I like her,' she said. 'Why?'

He shrugged. 'Oh, nothing really. I wondered if it was just me.'

'Just you?' she laughed. 'She's a very nice person and an excellent occupational therapist. Everyone likes her—everyone here, anyway.' She peered at his heightened colour and asked, 'Is there any particular reason for asking?'

He shook his head. 'I wanted to ask your advice. If—if I asked her out one evening, do you think she'd say yes?'

Caryn began to understand. 'I'm pretty sure she would.'

'Yes, but I mean—would she say yes because she wanted to go, or because she wouldn't know how to refuse?'

'I honestly think she'd want to go out with you, Pete,' Caryn said gently. 'And if you really want to know, I also think she could handle a refusal if she needed to.'

He grinned. 'Thanks. It was only a hypothetical question, of course.'

Caryn grinned. 'Oh, naturally.'

At that moment there was a tap on the door and Peter called, 'Come in.'

When no one appeared Caryn went to the door. Opening it, she found Helen standing hesitantly outside. She looked past Caryn to where Peter sat at his desk and began to back away.

'Oh, it's all right, Miss Dean—er—Caryn. I thought I might catch you alone.'

Peter began to propel his chair towards the door.

'I have to go now,' he said, 'so if you want to talk in here please feel free.'

Helen watched as he made his way down the hall, her face wistful. 'He's nice, isn't he?'

Caryn smiled. 'Well, I quite like him, except when he's being the bossy big brother.'

'I never had a brother,' Helen said, coming into the room and taking the chair Caryn offered. 'Just my dad and a sister two years older than me.'

Caryn looked up. 'I thought you said you had no family.'

'I haven't. I never go home any more—they don't want to know me. I think of myself as being alone.'

'And do you like that?'

Helen's eyes widened. 'I hate it. It's just that. . .' she frowned, picking at a loose thread on the sleeve of her sweater '. . .just that I don't seem to get on with people. They all find me repulsive.'

'Do you have any reason for saying that, Helen?' asked Caryn.

The girl sighed and her eyes misted. 'Everywhere I go, even at work, people seem to be in pairs. Oh, I don't really mean *couples*—like one of each sex. I don't even have any girlfriends either.' She looked up at Caryn. 'You must have noticed how Sarah shrank away from me.'

'That may not have been for the reason you think, Helen. Tell me, do you think you deserve to have friends?' Caryn asked.

Helen looked surprised. 'I try to be nice—friendly. I suppose it's like my dad said. Nobody likes a freak.'

'Your father said that—to you?'

Helen threw out her hands. 'He was always saying it; always trying to get me to lose weight. I've always been fat, you see, ever since I can remember. When I was in my teens I got really depressed about it. I tried really hard. But every time I got anything new to wear Dad would make me take it off. He'd say I looked ridiculous. If we had guests he'd give me money and send me off to the pictures. He was ashamed of me.'

'How did you feel when he did this, Helen?'

'At first I used to cry and hide myself away in the dark cinema. Then one day I got angry. Instead of going to the pictures I bought cream cakes with the money. I went to the park and I ate the lot.'

'Did you enjoy them?'

'Not really. I felt sick. What *did* feel good was the feeling that I was paying him back.'

'What happened then, Helen?'

'It went from bad to worse. The more Dad criticised, the more I ate—out of spite, I suppose. But then I couldn't seem to stop. I'd get depressed and unhappy and I'd eat. Then I'd feel guilty—look in the mirror— hate the way I looked. I'd try to stop. . .' She lifted her shoulders and looked appealingly at Caryn. 'I don't need to go on, do I?'

'No, you don't need to go on. I understand, Helen, but what made you come and tell me all this now?' Caryn asked.

'I had to tell you while I still felt strong enough. If

I'd slept on it I'd never have had the nerve. You see, talking this morning made me think, I've never really asked myself before how I got this way. I want to get better, Miss Dean. I want to be like other people.'

Caryn smiled. 'And you will, Helen. If you really want to, you will.'

When the weekend arrived Caryn found herself thinking of Adam and wondering when to expect him. He'd said nothing about when he would call—whether to expect a phone call. I hope he doesn't expect me to sit around waiting for him, she told herself irritably as she went about her daily chores. Perhaps he thinks I've got nothing better to do.

It was on Saturday afternoon that he suddenly put in an unannounced appearance. Caryn was once again tackling the unruly garden, wearing her jeans, wellington boots and a baggy sweatshirt.

'Hello, there.'

Caryn spun round, her face pink from exertion and her hair standing up in a spiky coronet. 'Oh, hello. I'd no idea you were coming today.' She brushed the dirt from her hands and straightened up. 'The garden goes mad at this time of year,' she added by way of explanation. 'Every time you turn your back the weeds have grown again.'

Adam frowned. 'I thought there was a gardener.'

'Oh, there is, but he's getting on a bit, and besides, he only comes once a week. It isn't enough to keep on top of it all.'

'Then you should get someone else to help him.'

Caryn gave him a wry smile. 'That may be the answer for people like you who don't have to budget for every penny.'

'Then please allow me. After all, I am your landlord, and——'

'*No.*' She cut him off in mid-sentence. 'Thank you, but we can manage. I quite like gardening, when I have the time. You needn't worry, I shan't neglect your property.' And she re-applied herself to her weeding with renewed vigour.

He watched her in silence for a moment, then asked, 'I admire your independence—and your energy, but are you thinking of taking a break at any time in the near future?'

'I'm sorry.' She stood up again. 'I don't mean to be rude—it's just. . .'

'That the garden has gone mad—I know. But I'm sure it can wait. *I'm* only here until tomorrow.' Adam took her arm firmly. 'Now, as a doctor I prescribe a nice warm shower, followed by a country walk and some interesting conversation with a friend. Later, a leisurely, candlelit dinner—for two, of course.'

'And who's going to take over my duties while all this is going on?' she asked.

He stopped to look down at her. 'Haven't you heard—it's Saturday afternoon.'

'Don't you realise, Mr Laine, that a lot of our clients come at the weekend? That's when we do most of our work.'

'So what are you doing out here?'

Caryn took her pager out of the pocket of her jeans. 'That's why I carry this thing round with me everywhere I go.'

He smiled coolly. 'I realised you might be busy, which is why I asked your brother if you were likely to be free. He told me that Saturday afternoon and evening is relaxation time for your clients; the period of time when they can choose whatever activity they wish to take part in—right?' He cocked an eyebrow at her. 'So you see, you don't really have a case for saying no, do you?' He grinned. 'And you can always bring your trusty pager.'

She laughed in spite of herself. 'All right, I walked right into that, didn't I?' They began to walk towards the lodge. 'By the way, I haven't said thanks for the roses yet. They were beautiful.'

'I'm glad you liked them.'

'But you shouldn't have sent them. There was no need.'

'I think there was. We did rather get off on the wrong foot, didn't we?'

'Maybe,' she agreed. 'But that was mostly my fault.'

'And your apology did you credit. I wanted to make my own contribution,' said Adam.

Caryn left him talking to Peter while she went off to shower and change. It appeared that the two men had the rest of her day planned for her, but she wasn't too upset at their collusion. Why shouldn't she enjoy an afternoon and evening off in the company of an attractive man? However, as she closed her bedroom door and began to peel off her gardening clothes she couldn't suppress a sneaky feeling that there must be a hidden snag somewhere in Adam's invitation.

In the bedroom she towelled her hair roughly and coaxed it into soft submission with the help of her hot-brush. After some minutes of contemplation in front of the wardrobe, she chose a light suit in a soft shade of green, teamed with a white shirt. It would be suitable for the country walk Adam had mentioned, and smart enough for dining out later—as long as he hadn't anywhere too smart in mind.

As she settled herself in the passenger-seat of the Porsche half an hour later she looked enquiringly at Adam. 'Where are we going?' she asked.

'Wait and see,' he said briefly. He was silent as they

drove along the coast road, and Caryn found herself
speculating once more on the reason for his invitation.

They had driven about five miles when he parked
the car on the cliff-top and turned to smile at her. 'Do
we really have a truce, Caryn?'

'Of course. I wouldn't be here if we didn't, would I?'

'That's good.' He looked thoughtful and she asked
hopefully,

'Does this mean that you've changed your mind
about letting us stay at Wessex House?'

He looked at her sharply. 'Why do you say that?'

She shrugged. 'Anything could have happened to a
man with your lifestyle, couldn't it? You might have
decided to get married, for instance.'

He drew his brows together in a guarded frown.
'Why should that affect Wessex House?'

She shrugged. 'You tell me.'

'And if it were as you say, would I be here with
you?'

She laughed. 'You might. It rather depends why we
are here, doesn't it?'

He shook his head. 'I'm not following this.'

'You want Peter, me and all our clients out of the
house by the autumn, and it seems that you have every
right legally to demand that we are. So why should you
bother to be nice to us—me?'

'Really, Caryn.' He sighed. 'It's hard to believe that
one as young and attractive as you could be so cynical.
You say you gave *me* the wrong impression. It seems
to me it was the other way round. I'm nothing like as
devious as you seem to think.'

'So if you don't have an ulterior motive, why am I
here?'

He laughed gently. 'It could be simply because I
asked you and you said yes.' His eyes searched hers.
'Well, couldn't it?'

'I suppose so,' she conceded.

'In which case, why don't we just enjoy the weather and each other's company and forget the psychoanalysis?'

Caryn had the distinct impression that she'd been outmanoeuvred. Adam had sidestepped her line of questioning so neatly that she was temporarily silenced.

He got out of the car and came round to open the passenger door for her. It was a bright afternoon with a soft breeze blowing off the sea. As they began to walk the scarf Caryn had tucked into the neck of her jacket worked free and streamed behind her and she felt her hair break free of its careful grooming to blow about her head in profusion, all her efforts to style it completely lost.

Adam looked at her and laughed. 'That's better. I like you windswept. You know, the first time I saw you you made me think of a bronze chrysanthemum.'

'Really?' She gave him a wry look. 'Thanks.' She caught at the scarf and drew it over the wayward mass, tying it under her chin. 'There, that'll fix it.'

They walked for a few moments in silence, then Adam asked, 'How are your clients progressing?'

'Quite well, actually.'

He shook his head. 'You know, I don't think I could bear it—having so little control, I mean. I like to be able to see immediate improvement when I work.'

'Surgeons usually do,' she agreed. 'Therapists need more patience.'

'Tell me more about your particular work.'

She glanced up at him sideways as they walked. 'Do you really want to hear, or are you just being polite?'

'I really want to hear,' he told her. 'It's something quite outside my field. Do you need any special qualifications for this work?'

'Training, of course. But more important than that,

I think you need to be a certain kind of person. Lisa—
Lisa Gregory, who trained me, told me that some
really first-class therapists fail in this work because they
can't conceal their personal revulsion for food
disorders.'

Adam nodded. 'Mmm, I can understand that—
particularly alcoholism. Maybe it's because they all
signify weakness.'

'All sickness must surely be classed as weakness,'
Caryn said quietly.

'No.' He turned to look at her. 'There are those who
fight, and those who give in.'

'Surely it depends on the cause? Some of my clients
have deep psychological scars—scars they haven't even
recognised themselves.'

For a moment they stared at each other. Adam's
eyes flickered for an instant with an expression she
hadn't time to interpret, then he smiled and took her
hand, pulling it through his arm. 'We're getting too
serious. This is supposed to be time off—for both of
us. We're here to enjoy ourselves.'

They walked along the beach for a couple of miles,
then scrambled up by a path hewn out of the soft
sandstone to walk back along the cliff. In the car Adam
reached into the back and brought out a basket con-
taining a flask of hot tea and two mugs.

'I thought this might be welcome,' he said. 'There
are some biscuits in the basket too. Help yourself.' He
looked at her, then reached across and untied the scarf
that covered her hair. As it fell back the strong hair
sprang up again, and he laughed.

'Now we're back to the chrysanthemum again!'

Caryn's hand flew up defensively. 'I must look a
fright!' She rummaged in her bag for a comb, but he
put out a hand to stop her.

'No, don't. It looks lovely just like that. I told you, like a——'

Her eyes flashed a warning. 'If you say like a bronze chrysanthemum just once more. . .'

'Yes, what?' His hand caught her chin and his eyes challenged hers dancingly. 'What will you do?'

His eyes pierced hers and she tried to break from his firm grasp, but found that she couldn't. 'What—what are you staring at me like that for?'

'I was wondering—if I were to kiss you again, would you react in the same way as last time?'

Her heart began to quicken. 'I—don't know.'

'Mmm. . .' He moved closer. 'I rather think it just *might* be worth risking.' His lips covered hers in a gentle, experimental kiss, and he gave a little murmur of satisfaction. 'Mmm, that was a distinct improvement on the last time.' He looked into her eyes. 'And I have a feeling it could get even better, given the chance.'

Caryn moved away, disquieted by the thudding of her heart. For once she would have given anything for the bleep of her pager. 'I think—maybe we should go back now,' she muttered.

'Not a chance.' He switched on the ignition decisively. 'I asked you out to dinner and dinner you shall have, if I have to abduct you to get you there.'

They drove inland to eat at a small riverside pub with a restaurant attached. Although it was small and unpretentious, the food and wine were good. During the meal Caryn began to feel more relaxed. Adam was very attractive. He was attentive too, making sure she had everything she liked best from the menu. They drank their coffee outside, sitting at one of the little wrought-iron tables on a terrace overlooking the water. It was still quite warm, and the swans and other water fowl swam close to the bank, looking for titbits. As

Caryn stirred her coffee Adam said suddenly, 'There's something I want to ask you.'

'Ask away,' she invited. 'It's not like you to be hesitant.'

His eyebrows rose slightly. 'You feel you know me well enough to say that?'

'I know you well enough to know that beating about the bush isn't your style.'

'Ah.' He lifted his shoulders. 'This is slightly different, though—delicate.'

'Then you'd better take a deep breath and get it over with,' she said practically.

'You said you'd no romantic attachments.'

'That's right.'

'Neither have I. In actual fact, I made up my mind a long time ago not to become seriously attached to anyone.'

'Really? Any particular reason?'

'A *very* particular reason, as it happens, but that needn't concern you.'

'I take it there's some point to all this?'

'Yes.' Adam stirred his coffee thoughtfully for a moment, then, 'And I think I'd better come straight to it. How would you feel about becoming Mrs Adam Laine?'

She stared at him incredulously for a moment, then her startled eyes crinkled into a smile. 'Go on, I give up—what's the punch line?'

He winced. 'Oh, dear, I was afraid it might sound bizarre, but I happen to be in deadly earnest—never more so. Seriously, Caryn, what *would* you feel about such an arrangement?'

'*Arrangement*?' Her eyes searched his for a moment, then she gathered her scarf and bag together and stood up. 'I'd say you were trying to make a fool of me.' She looked at her watch. 'I really have been away from the house long enough. Will you take me home, please?'

He paid the bill, then followed her out to the car park in silence. In the car he turned to her. 'Caryn—look, I meant it. I'm not joking and I'm really not making a fool of anyone—except, it seems, myself.'

She looked at him, her stony expression fringed now with bewilderment. 'Perhaps you'd better explain yourself, Adam. I'm not very good at conundrums.'

'Of course.' He took a deep breath. 'Look, neither of us wants a romantic entanglement—right?'

'Right. As far as I'm concerned my career is the important thing now.'

'Exactly. Me too. But we *do* want Wessex House.'

'Yes. . .' Caryn turned to look at him. 'But what. . .'

'We get along quite tolerably. We like each other well enough, don't we?'

'Ye-es.'

His lips twitched. 'I could have wished for a slightly more positive response to that one—however. . . We respect one another too, I think?'

'Look, this is all very well, but none of those things is a basis for *marriage*.'

'It would be in this case. You see my aunt's solicitor has found a codicil to her will.' He paused to look into her eyes. 'Caryn, if I didn't feel you had integrity and dedication I wouldn't even tell you this. My aunt made a condition to my inheritance of Wessex House. If I don't move in and live there as a married man within the next twelve months, the house will be sold and the money given to charity.' He quickly placed his fingers against the outraged O of her mouth. 'No, wait. Let me finish. If you and I were to marry we could share the house. You could still run your clinic and I my convalescent home. If we don't, we both lose out.

Don't you see? This is the obvious solution for both of us.'

She stared at him for a long moment. 'And if I don't *want* to marry you?'

Adam sighed. 'It would only be a formality—to meet the terms of the will. After the year was up we could get an annulment.'

'And what *then*? How do I know that you wouldn't kick me out of Wessex House once you'd met the conditions of the will and inherited?'

He smiled wryly. 'You haven't got a very high opinion of me, have you? We'll have everything drawn up legally. I won't let you down, Caryn, and I'll see that you're suitably rewarded too. Maybe a cash settlement—payable to the Lisa Gregory trust fund if you like. That's something we can discuss later. But I promise you it will be all on a proper legal business footing.'

Caryn shook her head. 'You're forgetting something: I have Peter to consider. Where does he stand in all these plans of yours?'

'I'm not forgetting him at all. I shall need a good administrator, a manager to hold everything together, because I shan't have much time to spend here myself.' He looked at her. 'That's another thing in its favour as far as you're concerned. You wouldn't have to be bothered with me for much of the time.'

Caryn hunched her shoulders and sank lower in her seat. All her practical instincts told her that what he was suggesting, although unconventional, made perfectly good sense, so why did she feel so. . .? She frowned, searching for a way to describe the uneasy feelings churning away in the pit of her stomach. In any other circumstances she would have said she felt hurt and humiliated. Yet how could feelings like those be aroused by a man she barely knew making a business proposition?

She looked up as he suddenly turned the key in the ignition and the engine sprang to life. 'You need time to think about it,' he said. 'Obviously it isn't the kind of thing you can make an instant decision about. I'll be down again next weekend. You can give me your answer then.'

As they drove back to Wessex House Caryn was silent, confusedly tugging at the convoluted tangle of her emotions. Clearly Adam had given this a lot of thought. Clearly it must have been the reason he'd sent her the roses. And the kiss—the sensuous blending of mouths that had sent her head reeling in a way she had almost forgotten; had that been part of the softening-up process too? In retrospect she found it faintly insulting. After all, if it were all strictly business why did he feel he had to flatter her femininity? Try as she would, she couldn't lose the feeling that she'd been conned in the cheapest of ways. Inside her, anger, disappointment and indignation struggled for supremacy, and by the time they arrived at Wessex House she had already reached her decision. As Adam stopped the car outside the lodge she turned to him.

'I don't actually need any time to think about your proposition, Adam. I agree that it would be a perfectly practical solution to your problem, but I couldn't do it. I couldn't marry a man I don't—and never *could*— love.'

'*Love*?' He looked surprised. 'I told you, it would only be a formality. It wouldn't last for long and I wouldn't expect anything else from you. You said. . .'

But her face, when she turned to look at him, stopped him in mid-sentence.

'I'm sure you'll find someone else who'll be only too eager to fall in with your plans,' she said tightly. 'And

if you want Peter and me out of your house before the
date we agreed on, just let me know.'

'But—your clinic—your clients. . .?'

'I appreciate your concern, but we have several other
promising properties to look over,' she told him,
slamming the car door hard. 'Goodnight, Adam.
Thanks for the meal—and the roses. I'm only sorry
your time and money have been wasted.'

CHAPTER FIVE

SUNDAYS were always busy at Wessex House, and that weekend was no exception. Fred and Annie were both there to help, and Caryn was grateful. They had more than their usual quota of weekend clients, and to complicate matters Helen and Fleur seemed to have taken a violent dislike to each other. Caryn had mixed feelings about it. On the one hand she was glad to see the introspective Fleur coming out of her shell, but she didn't want an unpleasant atmosphere about the place.

She had little time to think about Adam or his 'business proposal'. She had vaguely wondered if he might look in before making the drive back to London. But it was eleven o'clock that night before she thought of it again and realised, with relief tinged with disappointment, that he wasn't going to put in an appearance.

Having finally finished for the day, she took her coffee into the office, hoping to unwind in the company of her brother. But to her dismay she found Peter slumped over some paperwork and looking very down in the mouth.

'Hello,' she said. 'Still working? I must say you look cheerful—what's up?'

He pushed the work into a drawer and reached gratefully for the mug of coffee she put on the desk. 'I thought work would take my mind off things, but it hasn't.'

'What things?' Caryn sat down opposite him.

He shrugged. 'Oh, I asked Jilly round last night for a drink, while you were out with Adam Laine.'

83

'And she couldn't come?' Caryn looked at him enquiringly.

'Oh, she came all right.'

'Then why the glum expression? Did you have a row or something?'

Peter lifted his shoulders helplessly. 'No, just the opposite. It's just. . .' He looked up at her despairingly. 'Oh, Caryn!'

She looked at his face and her heart ached for him. He'd fallen in love with the pretty occupational therapist. She might have guessed it would happen. As well as being an attractive girl, Jilly was an exceptionally nice person. She was popular with everyone, but when Peter had casually mentioned that he was thinking of asking her out Caryn had no idea that he felt so deeply.

'Does she know how you feel about her?' she asked.

He looked up at her defensively, but the protest died on his lips. He knew there was no fooling his sister. 'Of course not,' he said gruffly. 'I wouldn't dream of embarrassing her with something like that. It wouldn't be fair. It'd be really pathetic, expecting a girl like her to look twice at a—a poor bloody *cripple* like me.'

'You can just stop that.' Caryn's voice was unusually sharp as she swallowed the lump in her throat. 'Are you listening, Pete? I won't have you talking that way. You promised me ages ago not to say things like that again.'

He shook his head angrily. 'I know, but why try to pretend otherwise? It's what I am, and nothing is ever going to change it. Let's face it, if it wasn't for you and this place I wouldn't even have a job or a home. Even this is hanging in the balance. What girl would ever want to throw in her lot with me? Certainly not one like Jilly. She could have anyone she wanted.'

'Maybe she doesn't want anyone else. If you were to ask her——'

'Well, I'm not *going* to, and that's all about it,' he snapped. 'And if you ever dare to mention this conversation to her or anyone else, I'll——'

'All right—all *right*. Calm down, Pete. Have I ever gone blabbing your confidences to all and sundry?'

He shook his head miserably. 'Sorry. Look, let's forget it. I don't want to talk about it any more, OK?'

'OK.'

He took a deep breath and busied himself with a file that was on his desk. 'Did you get on all right with Laine, by the way?' he asked.

Caryn lowered her eyes. 'Yes.'

'Have a good time?'

'You could say that.'

'No more roses, I take it.' He looked up and grinned at her with the ghost of the old teasing twinkle in his eyes.

'No, no more roses.'

Later that night, lying in bed, Caryn thought about her conversation with Peter. Her own problems seemed to pale into insignificance compared to his. From what she had seen, Jilly was certainly fond of him. But were her feelings as deep as his? Somehow, without betraying his confidence, she would have to find out and try to help. Lying awake, she wondered what the future really held for her disabled brother. He would hate the thought of a marriage where his wife earned the bulk of their income. Anyway, she was pretty sure he would want a family. There was something else too; although she knew he was capable of looking after himself she knew she could never bring herself to leave him totally alone. Even if she fell in love again herself she would feel duty-bound to care for Peter.

Her heart ached as she remembered the way he had been before the accident: strong and athletic, keen on sport; so happy-go-lucky, so *involved* with life. To think that one fatal moment on a motorway could change a young man's life so drastically. When Peter was in hospital undergoing surgery she had sat in the hospital chapel, thinking and praying hard for his recovery. And she had felt so strongly that he would be all right. The feeling that had surged through her that afternoon had been so very positive, and her hunches were usually right, so how could it have let her down? True, he wasn't completely paralysed. He didn't have to spend all his time in a wheelchair, and they were both grateful for that. But he suffered a lot of pain; more, she knew, than he ever admitted to her. And his life was a mere existence compared to what he had known before.

Caryn turned over in bed, rearranging the pillow as she tried in vain to sleep. There *is* one way that you can help him, a small voice kept insisting at the back of her mind. If she were to agree to Adam's proposition Peter would have a better job than he had now, and on a permanent basis. But she had already turned the suggestion down. How could she go cap in hand to Adam now and say she had changed her mind? Even if she did she might be too late. He might have asked someone else. Well, what if he had? She turned over again, punching her pillow viciously. There'd be no need for her to be humiliated. It was only a business proposition, after all, wasn't it? The first and most important thing was to find out discreetly how Jilly felt. And that would take some doing.

As it happened it was easier than she had imagined. On Monday morning Jilly arrived, bringing all her hobbies equipment in the hope of finding something to interest the three residents. Fleur was the easiest; she was already interested in art and turned out to be quite talented. It was just a matter of getting her to apply herself.

'Annie has come up with a good idea,' Caryn told the three women. 'She's suggested that if we could produce enough work she'd sell it in her craft shop and the money could go into our fund.' But the news lacked any great response, and later, as they shared a coffee together in the office, Caryn complained to Jilly about their lack of enthusiasm.

'Give them time,' Jilly said with a smile. 'At the moment it doesn't look as though their output will be very prolific, but once the bug bites them you might be surprised.'

'Well, if you say so. I have great faith in you,' Caryn said. 'I have a feeling that Sarah might take to it. It's said that bulimia occupies the "creative space". Sarah's fond of knitting at the moment, but that's more of a craft. She might respond well to being a little more stretched artistically.'

'Mmm, thanks for the tip,' Jilly said thoughtfully. 'I really must read up more on these eating disorders. There's a lot more to them than I thought.' She'd had her eye on the door all the time they'd been talking, and now she asked suddenly, 'Where's Peter? I haven't seen him this morning.'

'He's gone for his physio session,' Caryn told her.

'Oh, of course.' Jilly took a sip of her coffee and asked casually, 'Will he be back before I leave?'

'Probably not. Did you want to see him?'

Jilly looked unhappy. 'I'm afraid we had a bit of a misunderstanding on Saturday evening. He took something I said the wrong way.'

Caryn paused, unsure of whether to speak her mind or not. Then she said, 'Look, Jilly, I don't want you to think I'm prying into your privacy, but how do you really feel about Peter?' She hadn't meant to put it

quite so bluntly, and the moment the words were out
of her mouth she regretted them. How would *she* feel
if someone asked her a personal question like that?
But to her surprise Jilly looked almost relieved.

'I'm glad you asked me that, Caryn,' she said. 'I've
been wanting to talk to you about it for weeks. I'll be
perfectly frank. I'm very fond of him—perhaps too
fond. I've never met anyone quite like him, and I've
tried hard to let him see how I feel. But he holds me at
arm's length all the time. The thing is, I don't know
whether it's because he doesn't return my feelings, or
whether it's because of—what *he* sees as his disability.'

'Peter *is* disabled, Jilly,' Caryn said quietly. 'I think
that's something you have to come to terms with. He's
never going to walk or move normally again. He's
coped admirably with the situation, and he won't
tolerate people who are patronising.'

'Oh, but I'm *not*,' Jilly said quickly. 'Is that what he
thinks? Has he said so?'

Caryn shook her head. 'No. It's just that, particularly
in your case, he won't chance it. He's afraid to show
you how he feels in case you respond out of—well,
pity.'

Jilly stared at her increduously. '*Pity*? If he only
knew. Peter's everything I've ever found ideal in a
man, as well as being the only man I've ever really
loved.' She blushed and looked down at her hands. 'If
only I could find a way to tell—no, not just tell, *prove*
it to him. But even if I could find the right words I'm
afraid he wouldn't let me say them.' She shook her
head. 'I don't know what to do about it.'

Caryn smiled. 'Leave it to me. Maybe I can—how
shall I put it?—lay the foundations for you?'

Jilly looked a lot happier when she left, and after she
had gone Caryn went into the kitchen to help Maggie
with the lunch. As she stirred a pan of soup on the

stove her mind drifted. A 'business arrangement'—that was what Adam had said. Presumably she would stay on here and live at the lodge. But if Peter and Jilly married they would probably want to make the lodge their home. That was something she hadn't thought of. She would have to talk to Adam about it. There would be such a lot to think about. The legal arrangements— Adam had mentioned a cash settlement after the annulment, which would presumably be on the grounds of non-consummation?

'My goodness, Miss Dean, you do look hot!' Maggie exclaimed. 'I think we can start dishing up in a minute. Would you like a cool drink first?'

Caryn nodded, putting her hands to her burning cheeks, 'Thanks, Maggie, a cool drink would be lovely.' She couldn't tell the housekeeper that it was her thoughts and not the hot stove that was making her look flushed.

On Friday afternoon Mike came to give the week-enders their routine check-in and to check on the progress of the three residents. He was becoming quite an expert in eating disorders now, and they had recently offered to give a short informal lecture on Friday evenings, to talk about some of the less obvious side-effects of eating disorders.

This afternoon he was delighted to find that Fleur had put on weight. Only a couple of pounds, but it was encouraging. Although she still had little appetite she was managing to eat a little at each meal and keep it down. All three girls seemed well enough, though Helen had suffered a setback the previous evening, raiding the kitchen when everyone was in bed and demolishing the best part of Maggie's weekly super-market stock-up. Although Caryn had tried to keep the incident quiet Fleur had found out, and taunted the other girl relentlessly with it.

'Hail, Helen,' she had said, bowing low when Helen put in a late appearance looking bloated and pasty-faced. 'Hail to the fair Helen. The face that munched a thousand chips.'

Helen had slumped miserably in her corner and no one had laughed at the cruel joke. This afternoon Mike found her feeling dyspeptic and sorry for herself. He gave her a gentle lecture about the physical harm she was doing to her body, but, as he told Caryn afterwards, it was the fact that she had spoiled her record that seemed to worry her the most

'Your idea of encouraging them to keep a diary seems to work,' he said. 'It seems that even when it's for their eyes only that lapse is a reminder of their fall by the wayside.'

'Yes, when no one else is going to read it there's no point in deceit. That's a lesson that seems to go home quite quickly,' Caryn agreed. 'But on the plus side, they know they'll be able to turn the page over at the end of the week, and a new start is always encouraging.' She frowned. 'I wish I could get Sarah to talk to me, though. She seems pleasant and open on the surface, but I sense that she's still very tightly coiled inside herself.'

'I'm sure she'll loosen up,' Mike said with a smile, 'given time and your particular kind of persuasion.'

'I hope you're right.' She glanced at him. 'By the way, is Adam coming down this weekend?'

'Oh, yes.' He was busy writing Helen a prescription for bismuth and Caryn was grateful that she didn't have to meet his eyes. 'His outline planning application came up at the local council meeting this week. He'll be eager to hear whether he's got permission or not.'

'I'd like to see him if he has a spare minute,' Caryn said. 'Would you pass on the message, please, Mike?'

'Right. I think he was planning to visit anyway.'

'He was?' She found herself blushing as he looked up.

'Yes. He's bringing an architect round to look at the house.' Mike frowned at her as he put away his prescription pad. 'Are you all right? You're looking a bit pale today.'

'Oh, am I? No. I'm fine, thanks.'

'Adam hasn't been upsetting you again, has he?'

'No, not at all.'

He stood up and came across to her. 'Caryn, what we spoke about on the night of your dinner party—it still stands. If ever you want to change your mind. . .'

'Please, Mike,' she shook her head, 'I'd rather not talk about that.'

'I know. I only wish you did.' He put his hands on her shoulders and looked down at her. 'All right, I won't mention it again. I just want you to know that I'm always here for you—any time you need me. Right?'

'Right. Thanks, Mike.' For a moment she was tempted to speak out, to tell him about Adam's *business arrangement*, and ask his opinion. But she couldn't. She knew deep down that it would hurt him to know that she was even considering it after she had turned down his proposal of marriage so adamantly.

As the evening approached Caryn found herself growing more and more nervous as she waited for the telephone to ring. But the time passed and bedtime came without a call from Adam. Saturday morning came, busy with the usual group therapy session and talk. She told Peter to fetch her if there was a call, but by lunchtime there had been nothing.

After lunch Sarah and Fleur decided to take their

painting equipment and go in search of a landscape to paint. Caryn was waving them off on hired bicycles when the familiar low-slung car appeared round the bend in the drive. Caryn was glad she had changed after lunch into a bright cotton print skirt and crisp white shirt. But she was shocked at the way her heart lurched at the sight of the familiar dark head.

'Hello, there.' It was only when Adam got out of the car that she noticed that he had someone with him—a woman. A tall, slim brunette in an impeccable dark grey suit unwound seemingly endless legs from the passenger-seat of the Porsche and stood surveying the house, one hand shading her eyes.

'This is Evadne Jessop.' Adam held out his hand. 'She's my architect, and she's full of wonderful ideas. Evadne, this is Caryn Dean, the present tenant.'

Caryn held out her hand to the tall good-looking girl. 'How do you do?' She looked at Adam. 'I expect you'd prefer to take Miss Jessop round by yourself. I'll have tea waiting in the office for you both when you've finished.'

As she busied herself in the kitchen with the tea she could hear the muffled sounds of their voices and footsteps as they toured the house. Looking out of the window as she carried the tray through to the office, she saw them walking across the garden, engrossed in conversation. Miss Jessop seemed to be describing a plan to Adam, waving her arms enthusiastically and pointing. Watching them, Caryn thought of what she had planned to say to Adam, and her heart sank along with her courage.

As they drank tea together Adam seemed pleased with himself. He outlined the plans he and the architect had been working on, but Caryn barely heard what he was saying. She had screwed up her courage and now she couldn't say what she had planned. How could she, when they weren't alone? The conversation seemed to go on interminably. She vaguely registered phrases like 'pre-stressed concrete' and 'RSJ'. Asked for her opinion, she occasionally nodded and made affirmative noises, but all the time she was thinking that Adam would be gone soon—without her having had the chance to make her carefully rehearsed courageous speech. She couldn't leave it till his next visit. Anything could have happened by then.

It was almost four o'clock when Evadne said, 'If you don't mind, I'd rather like to walk round by myself. Is that all right?'

'Of course. Please do.' Adam went with her to the door. When she had gone he turned to smile at Caryn. 'I was really lucky to get her between jobs. She specialises in this kind of work. She won an award last year for her design of a new hospital in Wales.'

'Really? Good.'

'The outline planning permission to convert went through all right, though of course we aren't allowed to change the façade of the building. All we have to do now is to present a set of sensitive plans, to show them that we're not about to turn the place into an eyesore.'

'I see. It seems odd that you're not allowed to do as you like with your own property, doesn't it?' commented Caryn.

'Ah, but it's listed, you see. Grade Two.' Adam sat down opposite her and studied her face thoughtfully. 'You seem preoccupied. You're not still annoyed with me, are you?'

'What? Oh, no.'

'My suggestion clearly upset you.'

'No, it's all right,' she insisted.

'What's wrong, Caryn? Is there a problem of some kind?'

'No.' She took a deep breath. 'It's just that I—I've got something I need to discuss with you.'

He raised an eyebrow. 'Oh, dear. Sounds ominous.'

'No, it's—Adam, I. . .'

'No.' He held up his hand. 'Not now. Clearly it's important to you, and this isn't the time or the place. We'll talk about it later over a drink. I'll pick you up at. . .' He looked at his watch. 'Shall we say nine o'clock? I'm taking Evadne out for an early dinner first.'

'Are you quite sure you can fit me in?' Caryn felt her cheeks burn. She hadn't meant to sound so acid. If she wasn't careful he'd get the idea that she was *jealous* or something.

'Oh, I think I can—just about.' His eyes were amused. 'She's driving back to London afterwards, so she won't want to be late.'

When the architect came back into the room her face was wreathed in smiles. 'This really is the most *beautiful* old house, Adam,' she said. 'I can't wait to begin work on it, and I feel confident we can convince the planning people that we can convert it perfectly without spoiling its character one bit.' She smiled at Caryn. 'Thank you so much for letting us tramp round, Miss Dean. And thank you for the tea.' She looked at Adam. 'Shall we go now?'

Caryn watched as they walked back to the car, Evadne still talking animatedly. Adam had his hand under her elbow as he handed her into the passenger-seat, and Caryn felt a pang of resentment. On second thoughts, she wasn't at all sure now that she could go through with it after all.

The car passed Fleur and Sarah as it reached the bend in the drive. As the girls cycled up to her Caryn noticed that Fleur looked tired.

'I hope you haven't been overdoing it,' she said anxiously.

'I'm afraid she has a little,' Sarah said. 'Maybe a nice warm bath and a lie down before dinner, eh, Fleur?'

The girl nodded and gave Caryn a grateful look. 'I don't know what I'd do without all of you,' she said. 'It's the only place I know where people don't fuss and make me feel like some kind of sick freak.'

As she walked away Sarah looked at Caryn. 'I managed to persuade her that if she was going to take up landscape painting she'd need energy. I even got her to eat some chocolate.'

Caryn gave her a meaningful look and she added quickly, 'Don't worry, only one small bar between the two of us. I'm being very good, I promise.'

'I believe you. And I'm delighted.'

'I'll go and put the bikes away now.' Sarah paused. 'Fleur was right, you know. I'm sure we all realise how lucky we are to have found you and this marvellous place. It's so relaxed here.' She paused again, and looked over her shoulder. 'By the way, I've been thinking about what you said—about talking. I'd like that some time.'

Caryn smiled. 'I'm always available. Just knock on my door whenever you feel like it. Or if I'm not around come down to the lodge—it's quiet there.'

Sarah smiled. 'Thanks, I will.'

Caryn watched her wheel the two bikes away and sighed. 'We all realise how lucky we are to have found you and this marvellous place,' she had said. How could they give up all they had worked for now? She'd *have* to talk to Adam. She'd have to tell him she'd co-operate with his plan. It was the only way.

Adam chose a tiny pub in a village along the coast. They sat in a quiet corner by the fireplace with glasses of local 'real' ale while the village darts team played noisily in the adjoining bar. Adam settled himself in his seat and looked at Caryn enquiringly.

'Well? I'm all yours. Fire away.'

Caryn took a deep draught of the smooth liquid and said, 'It's about your suggested solution to the problem of Wessex House.'

'I see.' He smiled encouragingly. 'Go on.'

'Well. . .' Her throat seemed suddenly dry and constricted and she paused to swallow hard. 'Well, I know I dismissed it out of hand, but. . .'

'But now you've had time to think and you can see that the idea has certain possibilities. Is that what you're trying to say?'

'Something like that, yes.'

He smiled. 'Well, I'm delighted to hear it.'

'I thought I might be too late—that you might have asked anyone else.'

He looked surprised. 'Of course not. Who else *could* I ask?'

'I wouldn't know that.'

He drank the last of his ale. 'You're the only person it applies to.' He laughed. 'And I'm sure all my other women friends would be deeply affronted if I asked them to marry me just to solve a problem.' He pointed to her empty glass. 'Another one of those, or would you like something different?'

'No, no more for me, thank you.' Watching him walk to the bar, Caryn digested his last remark. Did he really believe that she had no feelings? Did he think her so plain that he imagined this was her only chance of marriage? And how many 'other women friends' did he have? As he sat down again she said,

'I'm only agreeing to this arrangement because of the house and the clinic, remember. And because of Peter, of course. His future prospects are so precarious,

Four Irresistible
Temptations
FREE!

PLUS A MYSTERY GIFT

Temptations offer you all the age-old passion and tenderness of romance, now experienced through very contemporary relationships.

And to introduce to you this powerful and highly charged series, we'll send you **four Temptation romances** absolutely **FREE** when you complete and return this card.

We're so confident that you'll enjoy Temptations that we'll also reserve a subscription to our Reader Service, for you; which means that you'll enjoy...

FOUR BRAND NEW NOVELS - sent direct to you each month (before they're available in the shops).

FREE POSTAGE AND PACKING - we pay all the extras.

FREE MONTHLY NEWSLETTER - packed with special offers, competitions, authors news and much more...

CLAIM THESE GIFTS OVERLEAF

Free Books Certificate

YES! Please send me **four FREE Temptations** together with my **FREE gifts.** Please also reserve a special Reader Service subscription for me. If I decide to subscribe, I will receive four Temptation romances each month for just £7.00 postage and packing free. If I decide not to subscribe I shall write to you within 10 days. The free books and gifts are mine to keep in any case. **I understood that I am under no obligation whatsoever.** I may cancel or suspend my subscription at any time simply by writing to you. I am over 18 years of age.

MS/MRS/MISS/MR _____ 7A2T

ADDRESS _____

A Free Gift

Return this card now and we'll send you this cuddly Teddy Bear absolutely FREE together with...

A Mystery Gift

We all love mysteries, so as well as the FREE Teddy Bear there's an intriguing FREE gift specially for you.

NO
STAMP
NEEDED

MILLS & BOON
FREEPOST
P.O. BOX 236
CROYDON
CR9 9EL

and I've discovered since we last spoke that he'd like to get married himself.'

'Really? That's wonderful news.'

'But he mustn't know that I've made this arrangement on his account. He'd be horrified. In fact he'd probably do everything he could to stop the marriage going ahead.'

'I see. Well, we certainly can't have that. So I take it we'll have to pretend to be in love?'

Caryn blushed. 'Well—yes.'

'You and he are very close,' Adam continued. 'Tell me, are you sure you can convince him?'

She avoided his eyes. 'I'll just have to do my best.'

He took out his diary. 'Right, that's something we shall have to work on, but, for now, down to business. I suggest we make it as soon as possible, so that the structural alterations on the house can go ahead without delay. Could you make it on the twenty-fourth—a fortnight today?'

Caryn caught her breath. 'Well, it's very soon, but I suppose so.'

'Good. Now, do you want to come up to town or would you like it to be here?'

'Here, I think.'

'I agree. We could slip into Dorchester to the register office. You won't want a lot of guests, will you?'

'Oh, no. Just Peter, perhaps.'

'Of course. On the other hand, we don't want to make it look too casual, so perhaps I'd better lay on a little family lunch afterwards at a local hotel. I'll ask Mike along too.'

'Mike? Oh—must you?'

He frowned. 'I thought you and Mike were friends?'

'Yes, we are. Yes, of course you must invite him.' She winced inwardly. What on earth was Mike going to make of all this?

Adam made a note in his diary. 'I suppose for the sake of appearances we should really go on some sort of honeymoon.'

'Oh, I don't see why,' she said quickly. 'We could always say that neither of us had the time, which would be true.'

'You're right. No honeymoon.' He closed the diary and put it away, smiling at her. 'So it's all arranged.'

'Apart from the legal side,' she reminded him. 'As a matter of interest, how long do we have to stay married?'

'I'll ask my solicitor in London,' he said thoughtfully. 'I shan't mention any of this to old Haversham—he'd probably have a heart attack on the spot. I think the minimum period is three years—unless one of us is exceptionally depraved.' He glanced at her, his eyes dancing. 'I don't think either of us is likely to fill that requirement, though I dare say it could be arranged if the worst comes to the worst. Is the time element likely to cause you any problems?'

Caryn shook her head. 'I can't foresee any. What about you? Suppose you find during that time that you'd like to be married to someone else?'

He shook his head firmly. 'I made up my mind long ago not to embark on marriage. My parents made enough of a hash of it to put me off for life.'

'So being married to me could act as a kind of shield for you, as well as a convenient way of filling the requirements of your aunt's will?'

His eyebrow's rose. 'That's an unusually cynical comment. But you could well be right, for all that.' He leaned forward to touch her hand. 'I hope we can be good friends, Caryn. We shan't see all that much of each other—I'll see to that. It's only fair. But when we are together we might as well enjoy one another's company, don't you think?'

Her heart began to race. 'I don't see why not.'

'And of course, if we're to keep up appearances we'll have to appear to be fond of each other.'

'Naturally,' she agreed.

'That's all right, then.' He looked at his watch. 'Well, almost closing time. Perhaps I'd better be getting you home.'

In the car Caryn was silent. Thinking over what had been arranged, she had a curious unreal feeling. What was she doing? Never in her wildest dreams had she imagined herself planning a bizarre marriage like this. Would she regret it? And how would Peter and Mike react when they knew? She was going to have to employ all her acting skills to convince her brother that it was what she wanted. Wistfully, she remembered the wedding she had planned when she had been engaged to Richard—the ivory lace gown, the four bridesmaids. There was to have been a lavish reception and a honeymoon in the Bahamas. A feeling of extreme apprehension began to chill her. What had she done?

Adam drew up quietly outside the front door of the lodge and switched off the engine. 'Maybe I should be with you when you speak to Peter,' he said. Clearly he had been thinking too during the drive home.

Caryn shook her head. 'Better give me this week to get him used to the idea.'

'That's cutting it very fine. Besides, I feel it would only be correct for me to. . .' he gave her a wry smile, 'well, ask for your hand, as it were.'

She couldn't conceal her amusement. 'I'm learning things about you. I'd never had you down for the old-fashioned type.'

'We don't know much about each other, do we, Caryn? I dare say we'll have a lot to learn about each other in the coming months.' He caught her chin as she turned away blushingly, making her look into his eyes.

'Caryn, we said we'd be friends, didn't we?' he said softly. 'Loving friends, I mean. If we're going to enter into this contract we might as well make it as tolerable as possible for ourselves.'

She avoided a direct answer. 'There's something else,' she said. 'Where are we to live when we're— after the wedding?'

'We needn't hurry to make a home, need we?' he said. 'After all, there are plenty of rooms here in the house, and you do have two bedrooms at the lodge.'

'Yes—two. But Peter has one, and. . .' She trailed off awkwardly.

'We'll think about that nearer the time, eh?' Adam bent and brushed his lips across hers. 'Now off you go and get your sleep. Tomorrow you have a bombshell to drop, remember? I'll be here to help you after lunch, if that's all right?'

She got out of the car and watched as he turned and drove out through the gates. It was done. She was about to become Mrs Adam Laine. A marriage without romance, without a white dress and bridesmaids—a marriage without love that was doomed to end in divorce at the first possible opportunity. What could be more arid? And why should Adam's casual attitude about it make her feel so bleak?

CHAPTER SIX

'WHAT on earth do you *mean*, you're marrying Adam Laine?' Peter's face was a study in outrage. It was seven o'clock the following morning, and he sat up in bed clutching the cup of tea Caryn had just brought him. 'Have you taken leave of your senses or something?'

'Of course I haven't,' she said as calmly as she could. 'We've been out together several times. We're not total strangers.'

'Rubbish. You hardly know him,' Peter protested. 'Only the other day you were saying you loathed the man and hoped we wouldn't see too much of him during the next few months. *Now* I hear that you're planning to *marry* him. It's ludicrous.'

Caryn shrugged. 'That's romance for you. When Cupid's dart strikes. . .'

'*Cupid's dart*?' He stared at her askance. 'Now I know you're off your head. When did *you* ever use an expression like that?' He threw back the bedclothes and began to struggle out of bed. 'I'm going to ring him right away and ask him to come round here and explain himself. This is ridiculous.'

She pushed him back against the pillows. 'Just hold on, you're doing nothing of the kind. First of all, I'm a grown woman, not a ten-year-old. And secondly, Adam is coming round to see you this afternoon anyway.'

'See me? What for?' he demanded.

She frowned. 'What for? To ask your permission, of course.'

101

'I hope you don't imagine I'm going to give it.'

'You can do whatever you like. We shall still be married.'

Peter started to say something else, then leaned back exhaustedly, pushing a hand through his tousled hair. 'Oh, come on, Caryn, what *is* this all about? It just doesn't make sense.'

'It's perfectly simple. Adam and I—love each other.' She spread her hands. 'It hit us both quite suddenly— just like that. You know how these things can happen. And we intend to be married—soon.'

'How soon?'

She moistened her dry lips She'd known it wouldn't be easy, but it was even harder than she'd thought. 'A week next Saturday, actually.'

'*What*?' He stared at her aghast. 'Look, I don't care what you say, you can't have thought this through. What happens to the clinic? I mean, if you're marrying him, presumably you'll be off to London. Where does that leave our project?'

'Well, if that's all that's worrying you I can put your mind at rest,' said Caryn. 'I've no intention of going to London. I'll be staying right here. We'll share the house. Adam will turn his half into the convalescent home he's planning and we can have the other half for our clinic. Did you really think I hadn't thought of you?'

'Well. . .' He looked slightly mollified. 'It didn't occur to you to consult me in all this, though, did it?'

She sat down on the edge of his bed. 'Pete, I told you, Adam is coming to see you this afternoon. We'll thrash out all the details then.' She smiled at him. 'After all, be fair. You wouldn't have expected him to propose to me in front of you, would you?'

He sighed. 'I suppose not. But I still don't get it.

One minute you hate the man enough to thump him—the next. . .'

She got up quickly. 'That's the way the cookie crumbles, as they say. Look, this way it's possible that you and Jilly could have the lodge for your own home. Don't tell me you wouldn't like that?'

'I haven't even asked the girl to marry me yet,' he said glumly. 'And I'm not sure that I ever will.'

'She returns your feelings, Pete. I'm sure she does.'

'She might *think* she does. To some women invalids have a romantic aura. When I marry I want to be the strong half of the partnership, not a liability.'

She ruffled his hair affectionately. 'Liability my foot. You're just an incurable old chauvinist, Pete Dean.' She grinned at him. 'So it's all right, then, is it—about Adam and me? You will be nice to him this afternoon—welcome him as your prospective brother-in-law?'

He still looked far from certain. 'Are you honestly sure it's what you want?'

'Positive,' she told him.

'And you're really happy?'

'Ecstatic.'

In the bathroom Caryn closed the door and turned on the shower. Standing under the warm water, she heaved a sigh of relief and began to relax. It seemed that Peter had swallowed her story. He knew her better than anyone. If she could convince him that she was in love, she could convince anyone. As for Mike—he was something else. What she had to convince him of was quite a different matter.

The fact that Fleur's mother was due to visit her seemed to be having a depressing effect on the girl. When after breakfast she still hadn't put in an appearance Caryn went up to her room, only to find that she still hadn't dressed.

'Why don't you put on your jeans and this pretty blue sweater?' she suggested, taking it out of the wardrobe. 'Now that you've put on a little more weight it looks lovely on you. And it's just the colour of your eyes.'

'Whatever I wear she'll say I look a mess,' Fleur said unhappily. 'She always does. I've given up trying to please her.'

'I'm sure that isn't true,' Caryn said. 'She told me on the phone that she'd really missed you since you've been here. And she's so pleased that you're better.'

A glimmer of hope sprang into Fleur's eyes, but quickly faded again. 'Is she bringing *him* with her?' she asked.

'Who?'

'Pretty-boy Pierre. I can't *stand* him. He always looks as though he's laughing at me—gloating.'

'She didn't say.' Caryn privately hoped the woman would come alone. She wished she'd thought to ask her now, but it was too late. Mrs Mason would have already started on the journey from London.

She arrived at midday, parking her white Mercedes sports car outside the front door, and as Caryn glanced out of the office window she was relieved to see that she was alone. Impeccably turned out in a designer suit, her blonde hair exquisitely dressed, Lysette Mason walked up the steps and rang the bell. As Caryn went to let her in she found Fleur hanging nervously around in the hall. She was wearing jeans and the blue sweater.

'Wouldn't you like to open the door to your mother yourself?' she invited. The girl shook her head.

'No—you go. I'll wait in the lounge.'

Mrs Mason greeted Caryn effusively. 'My *dear*, how nice to see you!'

'I hope you had a good journey, Mrs Mason,' Caryn said. 'Fleur's in the lounge. She's been looking forward to your visit so much.'

'Well, it hasn't been easy, I can tell you. In my job there's no such thing as a weekend.' Mrs Mason flashed her dazzling smile in Caryn's direction. 'Only last week we were in Italy on an assignment for beachwear. The week before, it was the Outer Hebrides, modelling a new knitwear range for one of the top houses.' She shivered affectedly. 'It was *freezing*. My dear, I can't tell you how we all suffered.'

'Before you leave this afternoon, Mrs Mason, I wonder if we might have a private talk?' said Caryn.

The woman looked suprised. 'Fleur isn't worse, is she?'

'Oh, no. There are just one or two things I'd like to discuss with you. If you'd like to knock on the office door when you're ready.'

'Of course. I was going to take Fleur out to lunch— if I can get her to eat any.'

'By all means,' Caryn said, leading the way. 'And I think you might be surprised on that count. Anyway, now you're here I'm sure you must be dying for a coffee. I'll get you one right away.'

'Oh.' The woman pouted. 'I suppose you wouldn't have a *teeny* G and T?'

Caryn shook her head. 'We don't keep alcohol in the house—for obvious reasons.'

'Oh, well, coffee will have to do, then.'

In the lounge doorway Lysette Mason stopped in her tracks, looking at her daughter, who stood by the window. 'My God, Fleur, whatever possessed you to wear that baggy sweater? It makes you look like a scarecrow!'

Caryn's heart sank and she said quickly, 'The sweater was my suggestion—the colour is so lovely. Fleur's put on four pounds since you last saw her, Mrs Mason. Isn't that good?'

The woman shrugged dismissively. 'I can see that living down here at the back of beyond has done nothing for her dress sense. And your *hair*, child! Doesn't this hole in the ground boast a hairdresser, for God's sake? I've brought you some new clothes— they're in the car. The sooner we get you into something more becoming, the better.' She looked at Caryn. 'Get someone to fetch the suitcase for me, will you?'

'I'll see to it.' Seething, Caryn went out to the car. She estimated that the visit would put Fleur back at least two weeks if not more.

Caryn saw Fleur and her mother leave. The girl wore a red dress which accentuated her thinness and drained her of colour. As she took her place beside her mother in the Mercedes she glanced up at the office window. Caryn waved and smiled encouragingly, but her heart sank at the woeful expression on the girl's face.

Adam arrived soon after lunch and went into the office where Peter was waiting for him. Caryn was hanging around in the hall, wondering whether to go in, when Fred appeared at her elbow.

'Where's the little flower?' he demanded.

He'd taken to calling Fleur 'the little flower'. Caryn smiled.

'Her mother came to visit for the day. She's taken her out to lunch.'

Fred's eyebrows rose. 'For a lass with a visit from her mother to look forward to she didn't look exactly overjoyed.'

Caryn sighed. 'I'm afraid she wasn't. In fact, between you and me, Fred, I get the feeling that Fleur's mother is the cause of ninety per cent of her trouble.'

'One of the pushy kind?' Fred asked perceptively. 'Expects too much?'

'Something like that. The girl seems to have had a good relationship with her father, but since the break-up of her parents' marriage. . .'

'Say no more.'

'Oh, Fred.' Caryn put her hand on his arm. 'I'm sorry. I know you——'

'Don't worry,' he smiled. 'I know only too well what divorce can do. Not that it isn't the best thing that can happen in some cases.' He looked at Caryn speculatively. 'Doesn't the lass ever get to see her dad?'

'I don't think so,' she told him. 'Maybe if he could be located. . .' She broke off. That could be the answer to Fleur's problem. She made a mental note to broach the subject with Mrs Mason later.

Adam and Peter were together behind the closed door of the office for what seemed to Caryn an interminable time. Eventually, unable to bear the suspense a moment longer, she made tea and took a tray along to the office. She found them seated on either side of the fireplace in earnest conversation. Both men looked up when she walked in, and she was relieved to see that they both looked pleasant and relaxed.

Adam rose to take the tray from her. 'Tea. Darling, how nice. Peter and I have been having an interesting talk about his accident and subsequent treatment.'

'Oh.' She looked from one to the other, wondering if that was all they'd talked about. Peter laughed, reading her thoughts.

'Don't look so crestfallen. We did mention you too— just in passing, of course.'

'Yes. Everything's arranged for a week on Saturday,' said Adam, slipping an arm round her shoulders. 'I'll be getting a special licence, and Mike's to be my best man.' He laughed. 'I've been trying to explain the "love at first sight" syndrome to Peter, but I've got a sneaking feeling he's known about us all the time.'

'In retrospect I suppose I did,' said Peter. 'It was all that aggro—a dead giveaway.'

Caryn poured the tea. So far, so good. She was acutely aware of Adam's eyes on her as he rose again to help her with the cups. As he passed she murmured out of the corner of her mouth,

'There's no need to overdo it.'

For an answer he bent and kissed her briefly on the lips, making her cheeks flare.

'Now *that's* something I thought I'd never see,' said Peter. 'My sister *blushing*.'

'I'm driving straight back to town when I've had this,' Adam said, sipping his tea. 'I told Mike not to expect me back. I had hoped we might have dinner together, darling—to celebrate our engagement. But I had a call at lunchtime. One of my patients is giving cause for anxiety and I may have to operate sooner than I'd intended. Maybe tonight.'

'One of the wealthier ones?' Caryn asked airily.

He shot her a sharp look. 'As a matter of fact he's an RTA victim—a spinal case. The operation could mean all the difference between complete recovery and paralysis.'

'I see.' She looked away, feeling slightly ashamed. 'Then you must go without delay.'

'I knew you'd understand.' He finished his tea and stood up. 'Come and see me off?'

'Of course.' She put her cup on the tray and went with him out to the drive. At the bottom of the steps he said, smiling, 'Your brother's watching from the window. Kiss me—and make it look convincing.'

She lifted her face to his and he drew her close, kissing her with what she felt was unnecessary thoroughness. Then he released her, got into the car and drove off with a cheery wave.

'Goodbye, darling, see you next weekend. Take care of yourself.'

Her head spinning, Caryn waved back and turned to see if Peter was waving too. But there was no one at the window, and when she went back into the house she found the office empty.

It was almost suppertime when Mrs Mason knocked on the office door. Caryn invited her in and asked her to sit down.

'I hope you've had a nice day with Fleur.'

The woman nodded non-committally.

'Do you find her improved?'

'I can't really say I do.' Mrs Mason took a cigarette out of her handbag and lit it, blowing out a cloud of smoke. 'In fact, if anything, she seems even more withdrawn than ever, and she hardly touched a morsel of lunch.'

'I wonder—have you ever considered family therapy?' Caryn asked.

'No, I have not. I think I know what's best for my daughter. This anorexia rubbish—it's sheer awkwardness—hunger strike. She's paying me back.'

'For what?' Caryn asked gently. 'Why should she want to do that?'

'Oh, I don't know. For being *me*. I suppose. She blames me for her father leaving, and of course she's insanely jealous of poor Pierre.'

'Is there any chance of Fleur seeing her father again?' Caryn asked.

'Only with the greatest difficulty. He's dead.'

'I didn't know. When was this?'

'Oh, about three years ago,' Mrs Mason said airily.

Caryn was shocked. 'Does Fleur know about this?'

'Of course she does. It's just something else for her
to blame me for. She blames me for everything—
because she failed at modelling and because she's no
good at anything else.' Mrs Mason stubbed out her
cigarette impatiently, seeming not to notice that she
was grinding it into Peter's pencil tray. 'It seems to me
that it's always mothers who get the blame when things
go wrong. It's so unfair.'

'That's why I thought that family therapy might
help,' Caryn explained. 'Their counsellors are used to
all these problems. I could put you in touch with——'

'Why *should* I submit to an intrusion into my privacy?' Mrs Mason demanded. 'I'm sick and tired of
being put under a microscope! After all, it isn't *me*
who's neurotic. It's high time Fleur pulled herself
together. It's just as I said—some silly sort of hunger
strike that's got completely out of hand.'

'But she *does* need help,' Caryn reminded her.
'Everything is being done for her medically and psychologically, but she needs help emotionally, Mrs Mason.
If you were to show that you care enough to go along
too——'

'I'm glad you think I have *time* to sit being preached
at by some do-gooder with a degree in sociology.' Mrs
Mason got to her feet. 'If this is the best you have to
offer, Miss Dean, then I shall have to contact Mrs
Gregory and tell her I'm not satisfied with Fleur's
progress,' she said. 'Not satisfied at all. Good evening.'
And with that parting shot she left, shutting the door
behind her with a bang.

Caryn sighed. Poor Fleur. If Mrs Mason's attitude
just now was anything to go by, the girl had had a
distressing day.

Mike arrived soon after supper. The moment Caryn saw
his face she knew she was in for an awkward interview.

'Is it true?' he asked without preamble.

'About Adam and me getting married?'

'Actually, I meant the bit about you being in love with each other?'

'If Adam said——' she began.

'Look Caryn,' Mike interrupted, 'I know my cousin. Even when we were kids I could always tell when he was being devious, and I smell something fishy in all this. I hope—oh, I *do* hope it isn't what I suspect it is.'

'Which is. . .?' Caryn's chin jutted defensively.

He sighed. 'That you're marrying him because of the clause in Aunt Grace's will. You are, aren't you? Oh, Caryn, you foolish girl. Don't do it—don't wreck your life. There are other houses. You'll find something else.'

'I have to do it, Mike,' she said decisively. 'It's more than just the house, although it's that too. We've talked it all through, and it's a sensible business arrangement. And the marriage part will only be a formality. We'll divorce the moment it's possible.'

He took her shoulders and drew her towards him. 'Are you doing this for Peter?'

'Partly—though he must never know that.' She looked up at him appealingly. 'Mike, promise me you'll *never* tell him, please.'

He shook his head impatiently. 'Of course I won't.'

'He's in love with Jilly, you see. He wants to marry her. We put all our money into this place, and he'd have no chance of marrying without a job. Adam has offered him a good one here as administrator; a home too. He's lost so much, Mike. It's a small enough sacrifice for me to make. But it isn't all sacrifice. I love my work here, and, anyway, I don't plan to marry anyone else.'

'I know you feel you'll never fall in love again—after what happened between you and Richard. But you can't do this—you can't cut yourself off. Suppose you meet someone else?'

'I won't. I don't want anyone else—*ever*.' She broke off at the wounded look in his eyes. 'Oh, Mike, I'm sorry.'

He shrugged. 'I'm sorry too—that I wasn't able to offer you enough materially. Maybe that way I might have got you instead of Adam.'

'You make me sound cold and calculating, Mike, and I'm not,' she protested.

'No. I know.' He stood looking down at her for a long moment. 'I suppose you know that Adam has asked me to be best man.' She said nothing and he added quietly, 'I wonder if you know what that's going to be like for me.'

'I'm sorry, Mike.' She was close to tears.

'Well, I won't pretend I approve, Caryn. For what it's worth, I think that what you're about to do is tantamount to sticking your head in the fire. For God's sake think about it. That's all I ask—just *think* about it while there's still time.'

He walked out, leaving the door swinging on its hinges. Dismayed, Caryn stared after him. Was there— could there be a grain of truth in what he had said? Could she really be playing with fire? She remembered the crushing pain of Richard's rejection, and thought uneasily about the way her head had spun when Adam kissed her this afternoon, about the heart-stopping tingling she felt when he was close to her. But that was no more than physical attraction, she told herself firmly. Love was once in a lifetime. It would never come again. Not for her. Mike couldn't understand that it was perfectly possible for two people of opposite sexes to embark on a business arrangement without becoming emotionally involved. But it was—wasn't it?'

* * *

Fleur was in her room with the door locked. After Caryn had tapped persistently and called her name for several minutes, the girl opened it reluctantly.

'Why can't you leave me alone?' she mumbled as she allowed Caryn inside.

It was clear that she had been crying, and Caryn saw that her supper tray lay untouched on the table. 'Fleur, this won't do,' she said. 'If you're going to slip back into not eating you know what will happen.'

'And who'll care about that?' The girl rounded on her. 'Look, I'll tell you something now. I've been eating since I've been here, right? Well, what you don't know is that I've been dosing myself too—so as not to put on weight.' She opened a drawer and felt at the back of it, producing some laxative tablets in a bottle. 'Here—you can buy these at any chemists.' She threw the bottle on to the bed in a triumphant geture. Caryn picked it up and looked at the label.

'On the little you've eaten these must have given you quite a lot of pain,' she observed. 'You realise, don't you, that you're storing up all kinds of health problems for yourself? Why, Fleur? Who were you paying back this time?'

The girl slumped on the bed. 'I'll never be any better now. And nobody really cares anyway. Being here doesn't help. Watching that pig Helen with her great fat face. And Sarah. . .what does *she* have to gripe about? She has a husband and two children who love her. They don't know what suffering is—either of them.'

'How do you know that, Fleur? Have you talked to them—really talked, I mean, not just sniped? Do you even *care*? Or are you so tangled up in your own needs that you can't see beyond them? Sometimes it helps to help others, you know; to give instead of trying to take from others what they haven't got to give you.'

'I wish Lysettte had never come today.' Fleur's eyes filled with tears. 'I wish she'd just leave me alone. I wish Daddy were here.'

Caryn took the weeping girl in her arms and held her. 'If you really feel that way, why not let go, Fleur?' she said gently. 'When I lost both my parents it was hard. I had to be strong and make my own life, build a career. You can do the same, once you've conquered this disorder of yours. Once you've finally accepted that you're a woman now and not a child.'

Fleur looked at her, her eyes enormous in her pale, thin face. 'I—I just want. . .'

'I know,' Caryn said. 'And you will. You'll be loved and accepted for the person you are. But first you have to work on that person, make her strong and positive and healthy.' The little red diary she gave all the Wessex House clients when they arrived was lying on Fleur's bedside table. Caryn picked it up and gave it to her. 'Write it in there, now, tonight. Make a resolution. Look on tomorrow as the first day of the rest of your life.' She pressed the little book into Fleur's hand. 'Goodnight. See you in the morning.'

Fleur smiled. 'Goodnight, Caryn—and thanks. I'll try—I really will.'

Maggie was really excited about the wedding. 'What will you wear?' she asked.

The question pulled Caryn up sharply. She hadn't given a thought to what she would wear to be married in. 'I don't know,' she admitted.

The housekeeper looked shocked. 'You don't *know*? I'd have thought it would be the only thing on your mind at the moment.'

Caryn smiled ruefully to herself. If Maggie only knew. Clothes really were the very last thing on her mind. However, now that it had been mentioned she

had to admit that something certainly must be done
about it.

'There's no one I can ask for advice,' she said
wistfully. Then, seeing Maggie's eager expression, she
asked, 'I suppose you wouldn't like to come with me?'

Maggie grinned from ear to ear. 'I thought you'd
never ask. When shall we go?'

They went the following day. Getting Annie to stand
in for her, Caryn drove with Maggie into Weymouth
where they treated themselves to lunch first, at a hotel
on the seafront. Then they set off to explore the shops.
Maggie had very good taste, Caryn discovered. In fact
it was she who took the ivory chiffon dress from the
rail and held it against Caryn, a dreamy look in her
eyes.

'Oh, do try this on—it suits your lovely colouring
perfectly. You could have apricot roses with it, and
maybe we could find some shoes to match.'

Left to her own devices, Caryn would never have
chosen anything so light and frothy. And she would
certainly never have described her colouring as 'lovely'.
Nevertheless, she tried the dress on, and had to admit
that it did seem to bring out the warm tones of her skin
and her hair flatteringly.

'Peaches and cream,' said Maggie delightedly as she
watched through the mirror. 'It might have been made
for you.'

They found a romantic wide-brimmed hat made in a
fine straw and trimmed with peach-coloured roses.
Sandals in peach kid and a handbag to match were
found at the next shop they visited. Much to Caryn's
relief, the whole outfit had taken a little over an hour
to find.

Over tea Maggie probed gently, asking about the
future, and for the first time Caryn realised that the
housekeeper might be worrying about her job.

'Nothing will change, Maggie,' she said reassuringly. 'Adam—Mr Laine will be converting the house so that it can be divided in two, half for his convalescent home and half for our clinic. I'm sure he'll be happy for you to continue as housekeeper.

'It's really amazing how well it's worked out, isn't it?' Maggie said innocently. 'And so romantic. It could have been disastrous if you and he hadn't liked each other.'

The morning of the wedding dawned bright and fine. Unable to sleep, Caryn was up early, making tea in the kitchen. As she sat at the kitchen table drinking it the enormity of what she was doing suddenly hit her. She had always believed in marriage for life. *Till death us do part.* Yet here she was, about to go through with a travesty in order to satisfy the whim of an old woman she had never met. Well, it won't be for long, she told herself through clenched teeth. Once the requirements have been satisfied we need see only the minimum of each other, and we'll divorce as soon as possible. In the meantime. . . But her mind blanked, refusing to think about the 'meantime'.

When she was dressed and ready she walked into the living-room, where Peter was waiting for her. Looking up from his chair, he caught his breath.

'*Caryn*! You look beautiful,' he said. Struggling to his feet, he crossed the room to her, leaning heavily on his stick. Standing in front of her, he looked anxiously into her eyes. 'Look, love, you *are* sure about this, aren't you? I mean, if you want to change your mind it still isn't too late.'

Caryn swallowed the lump in her throat and tried not to let him see that she was trembling. 'I'm fine, Pete, and I don't want to change my mind—honestly.' She took his arm. 'Shall we go? It's getting late.'

Adam and Mike were waiting when they arrived at the register office. Caryn dimly registered that Adam looked handsome and well groomed in a dark grey suit, but she was too busy trying to control her quivering knees to notice much else. Their turn came and the woman assistant registrar came to usher them in. The ceremony was perfunctory, and it seemed to Caryn no time at all before they were outside again, the register duly signed and the marriage certificate—formal proof of her new status—safe in her handbag. The whole thing seemed totally unreal to her.

Adam had booked a private room in a nearby hotel, where lunch was waiting and champagne was on ice. They sat down to lunch in an atmosphere of forced gaiety. Under the table Adam took her hand and squeezed it. She turned to look at him.

'Are you all right?' he asked. 'You have a sort of stunned look.'

'I'm fine. It just hasn't sunk in yet,' she told him. 'It all feels a bit like a dream.'

'Sure you don't mean nightmare?' He gave her a rueful smile. 'Don't worry, I'll try to make your awakening as gentle as possible,' he whispered, leaning close.

Her eyes widened. What did he mean by that? she wondered.

'You're making my sister blush again,' Peter said. 'But if she can't blush today then when can she?' He held up his glass. 'I suppose I should call her your wife now, shouldn't I?'

'I'll always be your sister, Pete,' Caryn said meaningfully. 'Nothing can ever change that.'

Toasts were drunk, Peter and Mike made brief speeches, and it was not until they were about to leave that Peter sprang his surprise.

'I've got something for you.' He put his hand into his

pocket and drew out a long envelope, giving it to Adam. Caryn peered over his shoulder.

'What is it?' she queried.

'You said you weren't having a honeymoon,' said Peter. 'I felt you should at least have a couple of nights away from it all. So I've booked you a room—the bridal suite, complete with four-poster, in a hotel in Bournemouth. It's only for the weekend, but I'm sure you'll enjoy it.' He looked at his sister's shocked face and added, 'And before you say you haven't packed, Caryn, I've done it for you—with Maggie's help, of course. Your case is in the boot of the car. Oh, and there's a present from the girls inside. Sarah gave it to me this morning. It's with their love.'

Crimson-faced, Caryn opened her mouth to protest, but Adam shot her a warning look.

'This is very thoughtful of you, Peter,' he said, taking the envelope. 'I can see I'm going to have the perfect brother-in-law.' He slipped an arm round Caryn's shoulders and pulled her close to his side. 'It's a lovely surprise, and I'm sure we'll have a wonderful time, won't we, darling?'

The hotel turned out to be a pink-washed wedding cake of a building, standing on the cliffs. The bridal suite lived up to its name—two luxuriously appointed rooms with an en-suite bathroom that was the last word in decadence. Caryn reflected that it must have cost Peter a fortune. If only she could have told him there was no need.

When the porter had left and they were alone she turned to Adam.

'I'm sorry about all this.'

He laughed. 'Why be sorry? Don't you fancy a luxury weekend? Or is it just my company you dread?'

She turned away to look out at the sea view. 'It isn't going to be easy, is it—keeping up the façade?'

He joined her at the long windows that led out on to the balcony. 'I'll tell you a secret; I'm not going to find it hard at all.' He took her shoulders and turned her to face him. 'You're looking particularly lovely today, Caryn. And to your credit, no one would ever guess at the sacrifice you're making.' He looked into her eyes for a long moment. 'Perhaps being married to me won't be as bad as all that. It's up to you really.'

'What does that mean?' She looked up at him.

He shrugged. 'It means that we have two alternatives over the coming months. We can ignore one another— or we can relax and enjoy the situation. After all, we don't get along so badly, do we? I find you very attractive, and I think you find me——'

She pushed him away angrily. 'If you mean what I think you mean, Adam, you can stop thinking it right now! Agreeing to marry you was the bargain, letting you take advantage of the situation is something else. Putting it bluntly, it's not on.'

He held up his hands in mock surrender. 'All right, I get the message, loud and clear, and I promise to behave. But there's no reason why we can't at least be friends, is there?'

'N-no,' she said warily.

'I mean, after all, it's going to be pretty bleak unless we can enjoy ourselves on *some* level, isn't it?'

'I suppose so,' she agreed.

'And just think—on Monday I'll be going back to London. Then you'll only have to see me at weekends. Even then I'll be too busy to spend much time with you. Should work out perfectly, shouldn't it?'

'Ye-es.'

'Right.' Adam dropped a chaste kiss on the top of her head. 'I'm going to have a swim in that pool we caught a glimpse of on the way up,' he said. 'When you've unpacked you can join me if you want to. Bye.'

When he'd gone Caryn opened her case. Peter and Maggie seemed to have thought of everything—even her swimsuit was in there, so she would be able to join Adam for a swim later, if she felt like it. At the bottom of the case was the present Peter had spoken of. It was from Sarah, Helen and Fleur, prettily wrapped in pink and silver paper and tied with silver ribbon. She opened it and took out the prettiest nightgown she had ever seen. Made of chiffon and lace in palest lilac, it lay across her arm like a wisp of cobweb. She sighed as she folded it away again, wishing she could have warned them not to waste their money. If only they had known.

CHAPTER SEVEN

CARYN was back at Wessex House by breakfast time on Monday morning. Adam dropped her off at the lodge before driving back to London. After waving him off she unpacked and changed, then made her way up to the house. She felt strangely disorientated. Just two days ago she had been Caryn Dean. Now she was Mrs Adam Laine, wife of a consultant orthopaedic surgeon, rapidly making a name for himself. Yet she knew little about her husband's background, or indeed about the man himself; had never been introduced into his circle of friends and probably never would be. She felt oddly anonymous, as though she existed only on paper.

Preparing to meet them all at the house, she adjusted her expression. She was supposed to be ecstatically happy, a new bride. She smiled wryly to herself. If only they could know what a mockery her 'honeymoon' had been.

She and Adam had been to the theatre on Saturday evening. By the time she had joined him downstairs at the pool he had booked the tickets, she assumed so that they wouldn't have to face the evening alone together. When they arrived back at the hotel they had a nightcap in the bar. Adam had smiled wryly at her as he watched her sip her drink.

'There's no need to look so nervous,' he said. 'I'm going to take a long walk when I've finished my drink. I don't expect to be back until late, but you can relax— I'll be very quiet when I come in, so I shan't disturb you.'

Upstairs, Caryn had undressed and slipped between

121

the silky sheets in the big four-poster bed. Eventually
she must have fallen asleep, and the next thing she
knew she was waking to find it light outside. On getting
up, she discovered that Adam had slept on the roomy
couch in the adjoining lounge. Last night the same
thing had happened.

Calling first on Peter in the office, she enquired if
anything had happened in her absence. He smiled.

'You're not indispensable, you know! Anyway,
you've only been away for thirty-six hours.' He looked
at her. 'Well, how was everything at the hotel?'

'Fine—great,' she told him enthusiastically. 'The
suite was beautiful. It must have cost the earth, Pete.
You really shouldn't have done it.'

'Of course I should,' he said gruffly. 'Only got one
sister, haven't I? Nothing but the best, eh?'

She went round the desk and kissed his cheek. 'Well,
it was a lovely thought. I—Adam and I appreciated it
very much.'

He glanced up at her. 'Happy?'

'Of course.'

'You're looking a bit tired.' He grinned. 'But then I
suppose that's to be expected.'

To hide her embarrassment, Caryn picked up the
morning post and began to look through it. 'Nothing
here for me. I suppose I might as well get started on
the group therapy session, then. See you later for
coffee.'

The three residents seemed much the same, although
this morning they seemed to be trying hard not to
bicker—perhaps for her sake. It seemed that Fred had
taken Fleur under his wing at the weekend. They'd
been walking on the cliffs and talking, Fleur told her,
though she seemed reluctant to reveal what they had
talked about. The other two talked about their weekend too. Helen was slightly down. It seemed she had

been at a loose end with the other two occupied—
Sarah had had a visit from her husband and sons.
Caryn noticed that, although she tried hard to appear
happy about seeing her family, she was jumpy and
nervous. Annie, who had stayed over in Caryn's
absence, had confided that Sarah had been heard in
the bathroom late last night vomiting. After the session
Caryn took her aside.

'Is anything wrong, Sarah?' she asked.

The smile vanished from the girl's face, revealing the
despair it had been hiding. 'Oh, Caryn, I'm no better.
Do you think I ever will be?'

'What do you think?' Caryn asked. 'What's troubling
you, Sarah? What is it that's holding you back from
letting us help you?'

The girl sank into a chair. 'Seeing Bob and the boys
yesterday I felt so bad. They seemed so pleased to see
me.'

'Of course they did. They love you.'

'I should be at home, looking after them. I might as
well be if this isn't working.' Sarah looked up at Caryn
with brimming eyes. 'I'm not worth loving, that's the
truth of it. I don't deserve them.'

'Why do you say that?'

Sarah opened her mouth to reply, then closed it
again. 'I expect you've heard that I spoilt my record
last night.'

'Did you?' Caryn laid a hand gently on Sarah's arm.
'You're not answerable to me for that, Sarah—I told
you when you first came here. *You* are the only person
who's going to be let down. It's up to you.' She
squeezed the girl's hand. 'When are we going to have
that talk? You don't have to make any soul-searching
revelations, just a chat. Tell as much or as little as you
want. Here at Wessex House you call the shots. It's all
up to you.'

'I know. And I *do* want to, I *really* do. You don't know how many times I've stood outside your door, about to knock. But I always chicken out.'

Caryn smiled. 'Well, maybe next time, eh? I'm always around, remember?'

As the weekend approached Caryn surprised herself several times looking forward eagerly to Adam's visit. She wakened early on Saturday morning, and although it was the last thing she had planned to do, she got up and spent the extra time washing her hair and taking special care with her appearance. Peter teased her gently over breakfast.

'Good heavens, I thought for a moment it must be my birthday or something. Then I remembered: Adam will be here in time for lunch, won't he?'

She'd lain awake for hours last night, wondering about the sleeping arrangements. In the confines of the lodge how would it be possible to conceal from Peter the fact that they were not sharing a room? But as it happened, he solved the problem for her.

'Oh, by the way,' he said as he reached for the toast, 'I've asked Maggie to make up the bed in one of the spare bedrooms up at the house. There's plenty of room at the moment.'

'Oh, Pete, I don't want to turn you out,' she said, trying to hide her relief.

'I insist. I'd feel in the way, intruding on the two of you here. After all, you're still on your honeymoon really, aren't you?' He grinned at her. 'Excited at the thought of seeing Adam again?'

She nodded, hoping her expression was one of happy anticipation. 'Naturally.' She looked at him. 'Pete, have you seen Jilly lately?'

He shook his head. 'No. What's the use, Caryn?

Letting myself get fond of her can only lead to heartbreak.'

'Why? If she feels the same. . .'

He frowned impatiently. 'Let it rest, Caryn. Newly-weds are always the same—they want everyone else neatly paired off. I've got enough to cope with. All right?'

Adam was late. Arriving after dinner that evening, he walked in on Caryn and Peter in the office as they were taking their coffee together. Caryn jumped up from the chair.

'Oh, Adam. I'm afraid we've had dinner, but Maggie can probably——'

'Don't worry, I stopped off for something on the way down.' He pulled her close and kissed her firmly on the lips. 'Darling, I've missed you so much. I meant to be here earlier, but I had a patient to see. We really will have to have a better arrangement. But we'll talk about that later.' He smiled at Peter. 'How's my favourite brother-in-law?'

Peter cleared his throat. 'I'm fine—but feeling distinctly in the way right now. If you'll excuse me. . .' He manoeuvred his wheelchair out from behind the desk and made for the door. 'Oh, by the way,' he said, looking over his shoulder, 'you'll be glad to hear that you've got the love-nest to yourselves for the weekend. I've made other arrangements.'

When he had gone Adam looked at Caryn's pink cheeks. 'Well, *well*. Whose idea was that?'

'His, of course. Anyway, it'll make things easier.'

'Will it?'

She shot him an irritated look. 'You know perfectly well what I mean.'

He shrugged. 'Unfortunately, I do. Is he staying with his girlfriend?'

Caryn shook her head. 'I don't think those two will ever get together.'

'Why not?'

'It's Peter's male pride. He says he won't ask her to look after an invalid.'

'But he isn't. At least. . .' Adam looked thoughtful. 'I'll have to see if I can talk some sense into that young man. Oh, by the way, I had a letter from old Haversham yesterday, congratulating us on our *nuptials*, as he called it.'

'So that makes it official, I suppose. The house is yours legally now.'

'That's right. I've also had Evadne's rough draft of the plans. I'll show them to you later.' Adam leaned back, one arm over the back of his chair. 'So—what are the plans for tonight?'

Her eyebrows rose. 'I wasn't sure that there were any.'

'*What*? The prodigal husband returns and you haven't made any plans to entertain him? I can see I shall have to get you properly trained.' He grinned mischievously. 'Or had you planned a cosy evening in, just the two of us?'

She sighed exasperatedly. 'Adam, you really don't have to put on a show. Peter's gone, so I don't know who you think you're impressing.'

Getting to his feet, he crossed the room to her, his eyes flashing with sudden anger. 'Caryn, for God's sake relax, can't you? Where's your sense of humour?' He grasped her shoulders. 'Look, you agreed to marry me—for our mutual benefit. You also agreed that we might as well be friends and make the best of it while it lasts. So what the hell is the matter with you? You're behaving like some sort of ice maiden.' His eyes narrowed and warmed as he looked down at her. 'And I've got a pretty good idea that you're far from that.'

'Oh?' She felt his eyes hold hers, almost hypnoti-cally, and found herself slightly breathless as she asked, 'And how—what gives you that idea?'

'Oh, the signs are there,' he said softly. 'The signs are all there.' He cupped her face with his hands and kissed her gently, then drew her close, pulling her defensively rigid body almost roughly against him and kissing her more deeply. He resisted her stiffness until he felt her begin to relax, allowing her body to mould itself to his.

'Oh, Caryn,' he breathed against her ear, 'isn't this much better than all that animosity? We could have some very pleasant times together, you know, if only you'd unbend a little.'

'I've already told you. . .'

'You tell me one thing with words,' he said softly, 'but quite another with your eyes and your lips.'

He kissed her again, and this time Caryn gave up fighting the battle that raged within her. As she closed her eyes it seemed to her that she was falling into a whirling vortex. Nothing mattered—nothing else even existed at that moment but the pleasurable sensation of his arms around her, his strong hard body holding her close and the relentlessness of his kiss.

A sudden loud knock on the door startled her, making her jump back from his arms. Adam drew in his breath sharply.

'Damn. Perfect timing. Who the hell is that?'

When Caryn opened the door Sarah stood there. She looked past Caryn at Adam and took a step backwards.

'Oh, I'm sorry—I didn't realise. I'll see you later.'

'No, don't go, Sarah.' Caryn turned to Adam. 'The key to the lodge is on the desk. If you want to go on down and unpack. . .'

He nodded resignedly. 'Right. I'll see you later.'

Caryn asked Sarah to sit down. 'Would you like

some coffee?' she asked, her hand on the still hot coffee pot. The other girl shook her head.

'No, thanks. Look, are you sure this isn't a bad time? I can always. . .'

Caryn put out a hand to stop her getting up. 'Just relax—there's plenty of time. You wanted to talk?'

'Yes.' Sarah moistened her lips. She was obviously nervous. 'Er—can I change my mind about the coffee, please?'

'Of course.' Caryn poured two cups. Sarah took hers and cupped her hands around it as though warming them. 'I've made up my mind to tell you something— something that no one else knows. Not even Bob.'

'Yes?' Caryn sipped her coffee. 'Take your time, Sarah. There's no need to hurry.'

'It happened a long time ago. I was only sixteen. My father died when I was twelve, and for a long time it was just my mother and me. Then she met Geoff. He was quite a bit younger than her, but she was crazy about him. He used to spend a lot of time at our house.' Sarah paused, pretending to sip her coffee, but Caryn noticed that her hands were trembling.

'And this Geoff—you didn't like him?'

Sarah's eyes met hers. 'No. There was always something—I don't know what. . . But although I told Mum she took no notice, and eventually they were married. Geoff was lazy. He lost his job and didn't bother to get another. He seemed content to lounge around the house all day and let Mum keep him. I was always home from school a couple of hours before Mum. I hated being alone in the house with him. He used to watch me—and—say things. Then one day. . .' She broke off and put down her cup. Taking out a handkerchief, she wiped her damp palms. 'One day he. . .' She caught her breath, her teeth catching at her lower lip to stop its trembling.

Caryn said, 'You needn't go on, Sarah—I can imagine. He raped you?'

Sarah gave a great shuddering sigh. 'It was bad enough keeping that locked up inside. But when I found out that I was pregnant. . .'

Caryn moved her chair closer and took Sarah's hand. 'What happened?'

'By the time I'd plucked up the courage to tell my mother it was too late to do anything about it.'

'You told her—about Geoff?'

'No. He threatened me—said he'd deny it, that it would be my word against his. He said Mum would never believe me anyway. I think he was right about that. She accused me of sleeping around—called me a slut. And the awful thing was, there wasn't a thing I could do or say to defend myself.'

'And the baby?' Caryn asked.

'I had a little girl. She was adopted. After she was born I didn't go home again. I couldn't have faced living in the same house with—with him. And Mum didn't really want me anyway. But I still feel so guilty, Caryn. I should have told her—told *someone* at least. I let it happen. I let Geoff get away with it, and I let my little daughter go to strangers.' She sighed. 'But worst of all is the lie I've lived ever since. Now you know why I say I don't deserve to be loved. I feel—feel so *bad* inside. Bad right through.'

'And when you vomit, you're trying to rid yourself of that bad feeling. Punishing yourself over and over,' Caryn said quietly. 'The cure to your bulimia is in your own hands. I think you know what the answer is now, don't you, Sarah?'

'Tell Bob, you mean?' She shook her head. 'I couldn't.'

'You don't trust him enough?'

'It's not that. I'm just so scared of losing him and the

boys. Why should he believe me any more than anyone else?'

'But you've never *told* anyone else?' Caryn pointed out. 'You're still listening to Geoff's voice—still believing his lies. You're still letting him win, Sarah. Look, you told me and I believe you. If Bob loves you, and I'm sure he does, he'll believe you too. He'll understand what you've been through, and it's my guess that he'll want to make it up to you. He wants you well again, doesn't he?'

'Yes.' Sarah shook her head. 'But how can I? Where do I start?'

'Tell him just as you told me,' Caryn said. 'If you want me to I'll speak to him first. I won't tell him anything, just prepare him. Think about it and let me know what you want.'

Sarah stood up shakily. 'Thanks for listening, Caryn.'

'Do you feel better for getting it off your chest?'

The other girl let out her breath on a deep sigh. 'Oh, yes. I can't tell you how much better. It's as though a great weight has been lifted from me. I'm sure I'll sleep tonight.'

At the lodge Adam had unpacked. Caryn found his things hanging in the wardrobe in her room, his hairbrush, shaver and toiletries on her dressing-table, but of Adam himself there was no sign. In the kitchen she made herself a sandwich and a cup of chocolate and carried the tray into Peter's room, closing the door behind her and quickly preparing for bed.

She fell asleep almost at once, wakening briefly as the front door slammed. There was a sound like someone bumping into a chair, followed by a muffled oath—then silence.

*   *   *

She awoke to the sensuous feeling of sunlight on her eyelids, but gradually she became aware that she was not alone. Opening her eyes, she saw Adam standing by the bed, looking down at her. He wore a dark blue silk dressing-gown and in his hand was a steaming cup, which he now put down on the beside table.

'So this is where you are.' He looked and sounded amused. 'I've brought you your morning tea, *madame*.' He sat down on the edge of the bed. 'If your brother knew you were sleeping in his bed I'm sure he'd be most annoyed, after letting us have the place to ourselves.'

'He wouldn't mind. Especially if he knew the circumstances.' It was the first time she had seen Adam unshaven and with his hair rumpled from sleep. For some reason it made him look younger and more approachable. On the two mornings they had stayed at the hotel he had showered and dressed before she was awake. She sat up, then, suddenly aware of the scantiness of her nightgown, she reached for her dressing-gown and pulled it around her shoulders. Adam laughed.

'Honestly. Anyone would think we were perfect strangers.'

'We might as well be.' Caryn sipped the hot tea. 'I don't really know the first thing about you. I was thinking only yesterday. . .'

'Oh, you do think about me occasionally, then?'

'Seriously—you know more about me than I do about you. I've never met any of your friends—your family. . .'

'There's no family—except Mike, of course. I told you, my mother ran out on me at an early age. My father—well, he had no time for his son. He had—other interests.'

'Such as?' she queried.

His face suddenly hardened. 'Such as a bottle—any old bottle as long as it wasn't an empty one.'

Caryn bit her lip. 'Oh, Adam, I'm sorry.'

'So now perhaps you can see why I haven't much sympathy with the over-indulgent clients who come here to dry out.' He made to get up, but she caught at his sleeve.

'Wait—that's not fair! There's more to it most of the time than mere drying out. When I was training with Lisa Gregory she was treating a young drug addict. His addiction started when he broke his leg. Morphine-based painkillers got into his system—got him hooked. But often there's an even more deeply rooted reason than that for their problems; a reason that basically has nothing at all to do with food, drink or drugs. For instance, you've met Fred, haven't you?'

'The little man who comes to help out at weekends?'

'Yes. He was once an alcoholic. He started drinking when he lost his wife suddenly. Later, because of it, he lost his only child too. But he beat it in the end, and now he tries to help others.'

Adam looked at her for a long moment, his face serious, then he smiled. 'You're a very dedicated, caring little person, aren't you?'

She looked away. 'Please, don't patronise me. And not so much of the little.'

'I didn't mean to patronise.' He took her hand. 'I'm sorry we missed each other last night, Caryn. As a matter of fact I got talking to Peter and somehow neither of us noticed the time.'

'To Peter?' She was surprised.

'I'm very interested in his injury,' he explained. 'I'm going to examine him today, and later I'd like him to come up to town, to my clinic, for some tests.'

'Why? He isn't ill?'

'No—on the contrary. I might be able to help him. I

have the feeling that the damaged nerves in his spine could well be treatable.'

'An operation?' Caryn queried.

'Surgery and therapy. I'll know better when I've had the result of the tests.' He smiled. 'Now, we only have today, so can we make up for the time we lost last night?'

'In what way?' she asked warily.

'What do you think? I want to show you Evadne's plans, for one thing. Then there's this complaint of yours—about not knowing much about me. Maybe we can put that right, eh?' He grinned. 'In the meantime, I'm starving. Isn't it one of a wife's jobs to make breakfast in the mornings?'

Later that morning Adam gave Peter a thorough examination, after which he announced that he was fairly sure he could help him. Peter was elated, but Caryn was a little apprehensive. Later, as she and Adam walked in the grounds, she said,

'You won't raise his hopes too much, will you? I couldn't bear him to be disappointed.'

'Thanks for the vote of confidence,' he grinned. 'Don't worry, I wouldn't say anything unless I was fairly sure. I've warned him that nothing's sure. And that all operations carry a certain risk, but I'm sure he knew that anyway.'

'It isn't that,' she said. 'Any operation that Peter had would have to be done under the NHS.'

He stared at her. 'You realise that might mean a delay—perhaps a lengthy one?'

'Of course. But I told you, we put everything we could raise into this place. There's no money for private treatment.'

'But Peter is my brother-in-law now.'

Caryn shook her head. 'I can tell you now that he'd

never allow you to let him jump the queue because of that.'

He shook his head impatiently. 'Caryn, the longer those nerves are trapped, the less chance there is of recovery. It's important that the operation is done soon. Listen. . .' He swung her round to face him. 'When you agreed to our marriage we talked of a cash settlement at the time of the divorce. Right?'

'Yes. But I——'

'If you're so determined to be independent, would you let me operate on Peter in lieu of that?'

She felt her heart lift. The thought of Peter, fit and well again, able to marry Jilly and live a normal life again. And to think she could do that for him! 'Oh, Adam,' she said delightedly, 'that would be wonderful.'

He smiled. 'Do you know something? This is the happiest I've ever seen you look. I'm glad there's *something* I can do to make you smile.'

As they toured the grounds, Adam described the plans for the conversion of Wessex House, pointing out the sites for the hydrotherapy pool and the gym, the sun-room and the covered play area.

'There'll be children, then?' Caryn asked.

He nodded. 'Oh, yes.'

'I take it you like them.'

He shrugged. 'I don't know much about them really, except as patients. I can't remember being a child myself.'

The telling remark made her look at him sharply, and she had a sudden insight into the lonely little boy he must have been. At boarding-school in term-time, then, because his father had little time to spend with him, packed off to spend the holidays with an eccentric old aunt. Suddenly she thought she saw the reason for the bizarre clause in Grace Laine's will.

'Your aunt obviously meant well,' she said. 'She wanted you to marry and have a family of your own,' she said thoughtfully. 'That's what she was aiming for when she made her will.' She looked at him. 'I'm sure she had your best interests at heart.'

He shrugged. 'Maybe.'

'In which case, don't you feel you're cheating her?'

Adam frowned. 'She shouldn't have tried to meddle. You can't manipulate other people's lives. If you do, you deserve to be cheated.'

Caryn stopped and turned to face him. 'And just what do you think you're doing to me, Adam? Or do you feel that you deserve to be cheated too?'

He looked at her for a long moment. 'It's not the same. I gave you the choice. ' He began to walk on, his eyes and mouth hard. 'What's marriage anyway? A contract, a bargain. The difference with us is that all our cards are on the table. We know how it will end, and when it does neither of us will be a loser.'

Caryn laughed drily. 'I think they call that hedging your bets.'

He lifted a shoulder casually. 'Whatever.'

'And yet you'd happily accept all the advantages of marriage—if I were to agree.'

He turned to look at her. 'Of course. Why not? We're both young, healthy and normal. What could be more natural?'

'And that doesn't seem at all cold and clinical to you?'

'Not at all.'

Caryn looked at him. She'd known he was cold and calculating from the first, but this was something else. 'And you don't feel it might be playing with fire? That there's a danger of one or both of us being hurt—when it all ends as it inevitably will?'

'Why should we be hurt? You're not telling me that

you believe in love and romance in these enlightened times? It's all an illusion, Caryn. Surely a modern, strong-minded young woman like you knows that? Gratitude and respect is the best one can expect from a human relationship. You give a little and take a little. Besides, we'll still have our business partnership whatever happens.'

'Maybe,' she said. Then, half to herself, 'But all the same, I'm not about to risk it.'

Adam took her arm as they resumed their walk. 'When Peter comes up for his tests, you must come with him and meet some of the patients who'll benefit from this place,' he said, abruptly changing the subject.

Caryn said nothing. The thought of meeting these pampered, spoilt children and their rich parents aroused no enthusiasm in her at all.

They had tea with Peter in the office, but when Adam announced that it was time to leave, Peter suddenly remembered something that needed his urgent attention. As the door closed behind him Adam smiled.

'The soul of tact, that brother of yours.'

'Little does he know,' Caryn said wryly. She looked at Adam. 'You'll drive carefully, won't you?'

He raised an eyebrow. 'You mean you actually *care* about my safety?'

'I care about everyone's safety on the roads.'

He shook his head at her. 'Never give an inch, do you? Except perhaps when I do this.' He drew her to him and kissed her. 'Apart from this house, this seems to be our only common ground so far, even if it does seem destined to remain chaste. Never mind, it's early days.' He grinned at her audaciously and kissed her again. 'Will you think of me when I've gone? Will you think about last night—and the opportunity we missed?'

'Not for an instant,' she assured him.

'What a pity. I shall,' he told her. And the way his eyes held hers brought the blood rushing to her cheeks. He was so wrong when he said that kissing was their 'common ground'. To Caryn there was nothing equal about it. Each kiss was more dangerous, more damaging to her defences than the last. And she knew that if she ever let him see that she wasn't the 'modern, strong-minded' young woman he took her for she would be lost.

As Adam drove away he watched Caryn's receding figure through his rear-view mirror with an oddly nostalgic sense of loss. There was really no need for him to come down to Dorset every weekend. In fact he was beginning to think it must be masochistic tendencies that brought him here. Each period of time he spent with Caryn was more frustrating than the last. The ceremony they had gone through together and the legal certificate that proclaimed them man and wife might as well not exist. But why did he care so much about it? he asked himself. After all, it was never meant to be any more than a business arrangement. As for her disappointing lack of response—he had plenty of young female colleagues who were only too willing to flatter his ego and share his leisure time. So why was it becoming so vitally important to him to arouse a spark of excitement in Caryn? An uncomfortable feeling deep inside told him that it was more than a mere bruised ego.

As he slid down the slip road and filtered the car into the motorway traffic he told himself resignedly that he wasn't sure any more that he'd ever succeed—that he was being less than fair to her in trying. She was a girl with integrity. He allowed his thoughts to linger wistfully for a moment on the small, piquant face, the huge green eyes and amazing bronze hair; the slender body that felt so good—so *right* in his arms. When Caryn gave herself it would only be to a man she truly loved, and who she was convinced loved her in return, because, for all her modern views, she still believed in love.

He sighed restlessly, feeling for the first time in his life a twinge of envy and discontent. It must be rather nice to be so näive—still to believe in that kind of ideal. In the past girlfriends who'd succumbed to the folly of falling in love with him had aroused no more than a feeling of irritated dismay. Many a happy and fulfilling relationship had been brought to an end by their tearful declarations. But now, all at once and to his utter astonishment, he found that the notion of having a girl like Caryn in love with him was just about the most desirable thing he could think of.

CHAPTER EIGHT

THE clients' diet at Wessex House had been specially worked out by Lisa Gregory. It was light and appetising, consisting of a high-protein content and with plenty of green vegetables, salads and fresh fruit. Right from the first day Helen had had difficulty in coming to terms with it. No more huge tubs of ice-cream, wolfed at a single sitting. No more doughnuts and pastries; no more thick white bread sandwiches, filled with jam or fish-paste. And most of all, no more chips. Potatoes were mostly boiled or baked in their skins. All bread was home-baked with wholemeal flour, and sandwich fillings tended to be of lean meat, cheese or banana.

Helen knew that she could easily go to the shops—although doing this would necessitate catching a bus into Dorchester—to buy treats. But she also knew that she would have to report such an excursion in the little red diary in her handbag, and this would ruin her own record of her progress.

She and Fleur had passed the stage of spitting insults at one another and had now settled down to a wary kind of tolerance. Helen saw that Fleur was putting on weight. Her growing friendship with Fred seemed to be helping her. Helen secretly wished she could find someone who liked her enough to call her 'friend'. She confided this wish to Caryn one morning, joining her for an early morning jog along the cliffs.

'It's always—been the same—ever since school,' she puffed as she pounded along beside Caryn. 'It's because I'm fat. Everyone hates fatness.'

'I'm not at all sure that you're right there,' Caryn

told her. 'Think about it; there've been some very successful fat actresses—even models. It seems to me that it's what *you* want that matters. If you're satisfied with your own body-size and you feel good about yourself, then others accept it.'

Helen stopped running to stare at her. 'You really think so?'

'I *know* so.' Caryn stopped running and nodded towards a bench. 'Let's sit down a minute.'

The two sat for a moment, regaining their breath, then Caryn said, 'I don't know if you realise it, but you've lost quite a bit of weight on the food we eat here. Have you weighed yourself lately?'

The other girl shook her head. 'Weighing is something I stopped doing long ago. My weight was always up and down like a see-saw. I'd diet and lose, then cheat and pack on more than ever.'

'Naturally. When you cut down on food your metabolism slows down, so when you start eating more again the body retains it longer and the weight goes back on.'

'It certainly did,' sighed Helen. 'And when the scales started zooming up again I'd get depressed—and when I got depressed, I stuffed. It was a vicious circle.'

Caryn smiled. 'I know. And that's why the right foods and a sensible pattern of eating makes more sense.'

'You know,' Helen said thoughtfully, 'I'm quite getting to like the food here now. It seems to help a lot. All those awful spots have gone and I don't get so many sore throats. Maybe I will weigh myself when we get back. I certainly couldn't have run this far in the old days.'

'There's something else you might like to give some thought to,' said Caryn. 'Do you really *want* to be thin?'

'Well; I've certainly never had any ambition to look

like Fleur,' Helen admitted. 'Not even now she's filled out a bit.'

'Exactly. Because you're not a thin type.' Caryn studied her. 'You know, you have a very pretty face now that the double chins have gone. Thin isn't always beautiful, in spite of all those magazine articles. Maybe this is your ideal size. Think about it, Helen. Stop aiming for what your father wanted. The choice is yours now, so, ask yourself, what do *you* really want?'

The other girl considered for a moment. 'Do you know? Now you mention it, I can't remember ever asking myself what it was I really wanted.'

'Well, it's time you did. You know, women are raised to feel they must please others first,' Caryn said. 'It's high time we asked ourselves what we want from life, I think.'

'And *I* think you're right.' Helen's face broke into its attractive dimpled smile. She stood up. 'Come on—race you back to Wessex House. I can't wait to get on those scales.'

Adam had asked Peter to think about going up to London for some tests, but Caryn knew he hadn't done anything about it. When she brought the subject up he shook his head.

'We can't both go and leave the place, can we? And I can't drive all that way.'

'You could go up with Adam.'

'And how would I get back? I wouldn't want to have to wait till the next weekend, especially once the builders have started work.'

Caryn gave the matter some thought over the next twenty-four hours, and when Jilly arrived to take her occupational therapy group the following day Caryn told her about Adam's findings and his proposal to do tests and possibly operate on Peter's spine. The girl's face lit up with hope.

'But he *must* go,' she said. 'I'd be more than happy to drive him. I could get a day off—if you think he'd let me go with him.'

'I suggest you ask him,' Caryn told her. 'And while you're at it, try to talk some sense into him. He thinks the world of you, Jilly, but he has this misguided notion that he's some kind of liability and he isn't going to be a burden to you.'

Jilly's normally serene face took on a determined look. 'I'll certainly try,' she said. 'I'm sick and tired of losing sleep over him. He's been avoiding me like the plague for weeks now—ever since we realised that what we felt for each other was more than friendship.' She grinned impishly. 'Maybe if I got him captive in my car for a couple of hours I'd be able to make him see sense.'

'Right—you're on. And I've got a better idea. Don't ask him first, we'll just go ahead and arrange it.' Caryn lifted the telephone and dialled the number of the clinic. Ten minutes later an appointment had been made for the following day.

Although Peter put up an argument he soon saw that he was outnumbered, and Caryn could see that he was secretly pleased and quite excited at the prospect of spending the day with Jilly. They left after an early breakfast, and all day Caryn's thoughts were with her brother. If only Adam could help him to a full recovery; though she reflected ironically that if she had known this was possible before it would have made her think twice before agreeing to marry Adam.

She had had a slight problem convincing Peter that the operation could be done without a lengthy wait. It had been necessary to tell a small white lie and to ask

Adam to back her up, but she felt confident that she had finally convinced him.

She was anxiously awaiting their return that evening when Mike arrived unexpectedly. Since the wedding she felt he had avoided her, but this evening he seemed his usual self. She made coffee for them both and carried the tray into the living-room at the lodge. The windows were open and the honey-and-spice scents of early summer drifted in on the still evening air. Mike sipped his coffee.

'It really is a lovely spot here,' he said.

'I know. I'll be sad to leave.'

He looked at her sharply. 'Leave? But surely you won't have to now?'

'Oh, only from the lodge. If Peter marries I'd like him to have this as his home,' she explained. 'And now that Adam sees a real possiblity of recovery for him, marriage for Peter and Jilly is on the cards.'

'I see. It seems that your marrying Adam has been beneficial all round,' said Mike.

A touch of bitterness in his tone made Caryn look up. 'You make it all sound so cold and calculated.'

'Well, isn't it?'

'I suppose I can't blame you for seeing it that way, Mike.'

'*Seeing*? You mean it isn't?' he queried.

She shrugged. 'It seemed the best thing all round. My marriage to Adam is only a formality. If we can all benefit it surely can't be bad.'

'So you've said.'

She met his eyes squarely. 'Yes. I won't allow it to be anything more than a formality. I've been hurt once, and I've no intention——'

'Of allowing Adam to hurt you,' he interrupted.

'Exactly.'

'Which, whether you like it or not, carries the

suggestion that you feel more for him than you'd have
us believe.'

Caryn sighed. He was in a strange mood this evening.
Her nerves were already stretched as she waited
anxiously for Peter's return. Mike's accusations were
something she could do without. 'What I feel or don't
feel for Adam is surely my problem, Mike,' she said
sharply.

He looked at her, holding her eyes for a long
moment. 'And it will certainly be that, Caryn,' he said
quietly. He reached for her hands. 'I wonder if you
know what it's like, watching someone you're fond of
leaping headlong into certain disaster.'

'There's nothing for you to worry about,' she
insisted. 'I can handle it. I. . .'

'*You're in love with him.*' The measured words and
the silence that followed them hung in the air like
smoke. 'I'm right—aren't I?' he said at last.

'No—no, of course not. If I——'

'If you weren't I'd have seen it in your eyes the
moment I said the words,' he said. 'Denial would have
been unnecessary.' He reached for the coffee-pot and
poured himself another cup. 'I was at your wedding,
Caryn, remember? I saw the way you looked at him
then. The expression in your eyes said it all. And I'm
convinced it wasn't all an act put on for the benefit of
Peter and me.' She started to protest, but he stopped
her with a hand on her arm. 'Caryn, look, I know it's
really none of my business, but I just want to warn
you. Don't start hoping and dreaming, because Adam
isn't capable of love. It isn't his fault. His mother left
when he was very young and his father rejected him.
He went to a very spartan boarding-school where they
taught total self-reliance. Even when he was a child it
wasn't possible to get close to him. He's brilliant at his
chosen career, and that's all that matters to him. He

does his job, and in return he gets gratitude, admiration and respect. They're all that matter to him, don't you see?'

Caryn was silent. Gratitude—respect. Adam himself had used the very same words. She forced a smile. 'Please don't worry about me, Mike,' she said. 'I've got myself together on this. I promise you I won't let things get out of hand.'

'Well, I hope you won't. . .' He broke off as a car was heard drawing up on the gravel outside. Caryn ran to the front door, opening it in time to see Jilly helping Peter out of the car. She was relieved to see him home again. And even more relieved to have her uncomfortable conversation with Mike brought to a close.

The tests had been intensive and tiring and Peter was all in after the drive back from London. He looked pale and exhausted, and he didn't protest much when Caryn insisted on an early night and served him supper in bed. When she had settled him she and Jilly sat down to talk over their own supper.

'Adam—Mr Laine seemed quite pleased with things so far,' Jilly told her. 'He's hoping to have more positive news for us when he comes down at the weekend.'

'Did you manage to talk to Peter?' Caryn asked. 'About more personal matters?'

'As a matter of fact, I took things into my own hands and proposed,' Jilly confessed, smiling shyly. 'I knew I had to do it now. If the test results are good it would have looked as though I was waiting for them. And if the news was bad it would have looked like pity. I wanted Peter to know that I love him and want to share my life with him whatever happens.'

'I hope he appreciates how lucky he is to have you,' Caryn said. 'What did he say?'

Jilly smiled reminiscently 'You know Peter—he refused to commit himself one way or the other. I expected that. But he made it clear that his dearest dream is to get well and for us to be married.'

'I'm so glad,' said Caryn, giving her a hug. 'But for now I suppose there's nothing for it but to be patient until Saturday.'

As it happened Saturday was an eventful day in more ways than one. The moment that Fred arrived to do his weekend stint at Wessex House he asked to see Caryn privately.

'What is it, Fred? You look quite serious,' she said, closing the office door.

'It's just that I might have to say goodbye in a few weeks' time.'

'Oh, dear, that is bad news. We shall all miss you, Fred. You've been a marvellous help to us here.' She looked at him. 'It's nothing we've done, I hope?'

He smiled. 'Far from it. I've come to look on you and Peter as family these past months, which is why I feel so guilty. You see, I'll be taking Annie with me when I go.'

Caryn stared at him. 'You mean that—you and Annie. . .'

He laughed. 'No, nothing like that. We're going into business together. We've decided to pool our savings and buy a little restaurant in Weymouth.' He smiled. 'I'm not getting any younger, and this is my last chance to make something of my life again.'

'That's great news, Fred. You know Peter and I wish you all the best of luck.'

'Thanks,' Fred smiled. 'I shall miss all of you and my weekend visits to Wessex House, and I know Annie will too. We've found helping out here very rewarding, and I hope we won't lose touch completely.' He glanced at her and she sensed that there was something else on his mind.

'What is it, Fred?' she asked. 'Is there some kind of problem?'

'Not really, though the restaurant isn't all I wanted to talk to you about,' he said. 'Fleur and I have been talking a lot lately. She's confided to me that she doesn't want to live with her mother any more. But obviously, to have her independence the child will need a job. I'm going to be needing an assistant and. . .' He looked up. 'Look—this might sound like cheek, but would you mind if I spent the next few weekends teaching her how to cook and present food? With Maggie's permission to use the kitchen, of course,' he added hurriedly.

Caryn stared at him. 'I think offering Fleur a job is a fantastic idea, Fred. But food—and *Fleur*. . . Do you think she could manage a job like that?'

'Believe me, I asked myself the same question,' he assured her. 'And I'm sure that with Annie's help she'll make it. She seems really keen. And don't forget it's a challenge for me too. I'll be applying for a licence— serving wines and so on. I don't have to tell you what that means to a reformed alcoholic.'

Caryn nodded. 'As you say, Fred—a challenge for all of you.'

'Exactly. We can help and encourage each other.' He smiled. 'Fleur's very artistic. She and Annie are full of ideas for the place—really clever things I'd never have thought of for myself,' he went on excitedly. 'And since the three of us have been talking about it and making plans Fleur really seems to have bucked up.'

'I've certainly noticed a change in her,' Caryn agreed.

'There's even a little flat over the place with a room

for each of us,' Fred went on. 'So she'll have privacy without having to live on her own.'

Caryn smiled. 'It all sounds ideal. And Fleur's certainly old enough to make her own decisions. Feel free to use the kitchen with my blessing.' She grinned. 'And, as you say—with Maggie's permission, of course.'

Adam arrived soon after lunch, and almost as soon as he arrived he announced that Peter's test results were through. Caryn's heart was beating fast as she waited expectantly.

'I'll come straight to the point,' he said. 'I know you must both be waiting to hear the prognosis.'

Peter looked outwardly calm. Only Caryn knew, from the tension in his hands as he clutched the sides of his chair, what he was really feeling. 'I've been trying not to think about it too much,' he said. 'After all, if the tests offer no hope I'll be no worse off than I am now, will I?'

'In fact, I hope you're going to be a great deal better off,' Adam said with a smile. 'All the tests point to what I suspected, and the results are positively in favour of surgery. I'm ninety-nine per cent certain that I can restore full use of your legs.'

'Oh, Pete, isn't that marvellous?' Caryn looked at her brother, but his expression was guarded.

'How long would I have to wait for the op?' he asked.

'Well,' Adam shot Caryn a look, 'as this isn't an operation I do very often I haven't many patients waiting. As a matter of fact, it would be more convenient for me if you came into the clinic to have it done. If you agree to that I can do it for you the week after next.'

Peter's eyes widened. 'That soon?' He looked at Caryn doubtfully. 'Oh, but what about this place?'

'Don't worry about that. I'll get on to Lisa,' she said decisively. 'I'm sure she'll send us someone to help out. I'll come up to London and stay until the op's over, then I'll come back.' She looked at Adam. 'How long will he be out of action?'

'Not too long. It'll be a matter of re-educating muscles that haven't been used for a while. Patience and plenty of physiotherapy should do it.'

The three looked at each other, momentarily lost for words, then Adam said, 'Is it agreed, then—the week after next?'

Peter nodded eagerly, his face flushed. 'Well, what do you think?' He grinned. 'I can hardly believe it.'

Caryn smiled. 'I dare say you'll be wanting to ring Jilly,' she said. 'She's been waiting on tenterhooks all week.' She glanced at Adam. 'We'll leave you alone, won't we, Adam?'

When they were outside Adam turned to look at her. 'Well, how has your week been?'

'Tense, mainly,' she told him. 'But strange too— transient almost. I feel as though I'm coming to the end of a chapter.'

'Oh? How's that?'

She glanced up at him as they walked. 'My three residents are almost ready to leave; Peter's to have his operation. Then there's this place. . .'

'Ah, yes—I meant to tell you,' he said. 'Evadne's coming down later this afternoon. We're to have a meeting with the builder. With luck they can begin on the work next week.'

'So that's another thing that's changing,' Caryn said.

'Don't you find it all exciting?'

She swallowed hard, avoiding his eyes. What she felt wasn't excitement. In a way that she didn't care to analyse, she felt that everyone else was moving on and she was being left behind.

'You don't look excited. In fact you look distinctly depressed. Why don't you come out to dinner this evening with Evadne and me? I've booked a table at a new place that I'm told is rather good.'

'I can't,' said Caryn. 'I've asked the husband of one of my residents to see me. I'll have to be available for him.'

Evadne arrived along with the Saturday afternoon visitors. As she went out to meet them Caryn saw the architect drive in in her racy little car. Adam walked out to open the door for her and she watched as he greeted Evadne warmly, throwing an arm across her shoulders as they set off on their tour of the house.

Swallowing the unexpectedly sharp pang she felt, Caryn turned away and applied her mind firmly to the afternoon's work.

Later that evening she saw Adam and Evadne drive off to their dinner date in Adam's car just as Bob Harris, Sarah's husband, arrived. By the time she got out to the drive Bob was locking his car. He turned to her, an apprehensive expression on his face.

She held out her hand. 'Good evening, Mr Harris. I'm glad you were able to get here. Did you have a good journey?'

'Yes, thank you, Miss Dean—I mean Mrs Laine.' He cleared his throat. 'Your telephone call worried me a bit. Is everything all right?'

'Nothing to worry about at all. But shall we go inside and sit down in comfort?'

In the office she smiled reassuringly. 'Please sit down, Mr Harris. And don't look so worried—it's not bad news.' When he was settled she said, 'Do you think Sarah's improved since she's been here?'

He looked uneasy. 'Well, sometimes I think she has, then at others—I just don't know.'

'You've had bulimia explained to you, haven't you?'

'Up to a point.'

'Psychologically, in vomiting the sufferer is trying to rid herself of something deep within herself. The patient isn't aware of this, of course, and it's often buried so deeply that the cause is hard to find. But if it can—and if she can be made aware of what it is she's trying to eliminate, she can be cured.'

'I see.'

'Sometimes the problem lies with a feeling of guilt over something in the past.'

The man looked up sharply. 'Are you saying that Sarah did something wrong?'

Caryn shook her head. 'Not at all. But she did have a traumatic experience, back in her extreme youth; something that hurt her very badly psychologically. She wants to tell you about it, but she's terribly afraid of how you'll take it.' She looked at the man gravely. 'Her whole future and well-being will depend on your reaction, Mr Harris, but I'm sure I don't have to tell you that.'

Bob frowned. 'Now you've really got me worried. We've always been completely honest with each other. Why has she never told me this before?'

'Because she's been trying to block it out all these years, trying to pretend it never happened. Maybe she hoped the memory would go away if she ignored it— who can really know?' said Caryn. 'But it didn't go away. It came back to haunt her in a different and terrible way.'

He shook his head. 'I still don't really understand. I'm her husband. Surely she knows I'll still love her, whatever happened in the past. Nothing could make any difference to that.'

Caryn smiled. 'I was hoping to hear you say that, Mr Harris. She's waiting for you now. Take her out in the car, somewhere quiet where you can be alone. Don't pressure her, let her tell you in her own time.' She got up and held out her hand. 'And the best of luck to you both. I have a feeling you'll soon be taking Sarah home with you again.'

From the office window she saw them get into the car a few minutes later and drive away. Deep inside she felt sure that Sarah's troubles were on the mend at last, and she sighed as she thought of her own impossible situation. She was so good at telling other people where they were going wrong, so why had she made such a mess of her own life? Aloud, she repeated what she had said to Helen: 'Ask yourself, what do you really want.' And: 'Women are raised to feel they must please others. . .it's high time we asked ourselves what we want from life.' She smiled wryly to herself. It was so easy to talk—to give advice.

She went back to sit at the desk, remembering Mike's words as she did so. He had accused her of being in love with Adam—of marrying him for all the wrong reasons. Well, it was true, even though she had denied it. It seemed that she was heading for another hurt, this time self-inflicted, deeper and more wounding than she had ever known. She took a deep breath and pulled the telephone towards her. Never mind that. Peter was the foremost person right now. His recovery was the important thing. At least that was something positive that would have resulted from her disastrous marriage to Adam. She must talk to Lisa at once about sending someone to stand in for her while they were away. She dialled the number and waited.

'Hello, Lisa Gregory speaking.'

'Lisa, it's me—Caryn.'

'Well, well, how nice to hear from you.'

'Lisa, I've got some rather exciting news. Peter's to have an operation in London the week after next. The consultant surgeon has almost guaranteed the full recovery of his legs. The thing is—I'd like to go up with him and stay, just until he's had the op. Would it be possible for you to send a replacement for a few days?'

There was a small silence at the other end of the telephone, then Lisa said, 'It's strange that you should ring, Caryn. I was going to get in touch with you. I want to talk to you about the future of Wessex House. I think that in the circumstances the best thing would be for me to come down there myself. Then we can talk face to face.'

Caryn's heart sank. *Face to face*. It sounded ominous. 'What is it, Lisa?' she asked apprehensively. 'Is something wrong?'

'We'll talk when we meet,' Lisa said dismissively. 'I'm delighted about Peter. Oh, and about your marriage, by the way—I had to hear about it on the grapevine. And you didn't invite me to the wedding either. I shall have to have some very stern words with you about that.'

'It was very quiet,' Caryn explained. 'Actually, Adam owns Wessex House.'

'I know.' Again there was a small silence, then Lisa said cheerfully, 'Well, we'll have a long talk when we meet, shall we? I'll join you next weekend if that's convenient.'

'Fine. I'll look forward to seeing you, Lisa.'

'Me too. Goodbye.'

When Caryn put down the phone she sat for a long time, wondering what Lisa had to tell her. How did she know that Adam was the new owner of Wessex House? She couldn't shake off the feeling of foreboding that filled her mind.

It was almost midnight when she returned to the lodge. Peter was already asleep, and Caryn took a shower and got ready for bed herself.

Adam hadn't come in. An hour later he still hadn't arrived, and Caryn lay awake, staring at the moonlit ceiling, trying not to ask herself where he was and what he could be doing. Presumably Evadne was more liberal in her views than she, and if she had invited Adam back to her hotel room why should he refuse? Had he told her about their marriage of convenience— their business arrangement? she wondered. What a fool Evadne must think her.

She was just drifting into an uneasy sleep when her pager began to bleep. Instantly she was wide awake, out of bed and pulling on jeans and a sweater.

Fleur sat on the front steps waiting for her, huddled in her dressing-gown.

'I'm sorry to wake you, Caryn,' she said.'I came out here because I didn't want to wake the whole house. I should have hung on till the morning, but my mind just kept going round and round like a mouse in a wheel, till my nerves were at screaming pitch. I *had* to talk to you.'

Caryn slipped an arm around the other girl's shoulders. 'Come in, you'll catch cold. We'll make some cocoa and talk in the kitchen.'

In the large old-fashioned kitchen Caryn stirred the Aga into life and filled the kettle. 'So tell me about it,' she invited, pulling two chairs close to the glowing range. 'Is it anything to do with Fred's offer?'

'Indirectly,' said Fleur. 'I was so thrilled when he offered me the job. It's a marvellous chance to make a new start, but not only that. I felt he must have real faith in me to make it. That meant everything to me.' She paused for breath. 'But that was before my mother came to visit this afternoon. . .' She broke off, looking down at the hands that were twisted together in her lap.

'You told her—and she didn't approve?' Caryn prompted.

'She sneered at it—made it all sound cheap and nasty,' said Fleur. '"Shacking up with some old lush" was how she described it. "Shovelling chips in a seaside caff". She wouldn't even let me introduce her to Fred, though I can't say I was sorry about that. She'd probably have been rude to him. She said I was weak and stupid. That I was obviously drawn to people who are as weak and feeble as I am, so as to feel—feel. . .'

Caryn reached out to touch her hand. 'Feel what, Fleur?'

'Among my own kind.' Fleur looked up at her with huge eyes. 'There, I've said it!' Her eyes filled with tears. 'She's done it again, Caryn. She's made me feel like a freak. She's spoiled it all for me—just like she spoils everything. She's made me see Fred's offer through her eyes. I don't know if I can go through with it now.'

The kettle boiled and Caryn rose to make the cocoa. As she handed the other girl her mug she sat down beside her. 'Fleur, don't you see? If you back out now you'll have let her win again.'

'But she's right in a way,' Fleur insisted. 'That's the way she gets me every time. There's always a grain of truth in what she says.'

'Of course there is. She's right in thinking that you need to be with someone who understands you,' Caryn said. 'And the fact that you've recognised that is a big step towards your recovery. When you first came you wouldn't make friends with anyone, would you?'

Fleur nodded. 'Because I hated the look in people's eyes. But Fred's different. He knows what it's like. He reminds me of—of. . .'

'Of your father?' Caryn said quietly.

Fleur looked up. 'How did you guess?'

Caryn smiled. 'I loved my father too. Look, think about it, Fleur. We all need someone—even the strongest person can't make it through life in complete isolation. Even your mother has Pierre. You're old enough to make your own mind up now. You don't have to listen to anyone. Find out for yourself. Go to work with Fred and Annie. Prove to your mother that you can make a go of it. Don't you see? It's an even greater challenge now. You've just *got* to meet it.'

Fleur went back to bed in a happier frame of mind, and Caryn set off down the drive again. Dawn was breaking, and as she reached the lodge the birds began their morning chorus. Outside the front door stood Adam's car. In the bedroom she found him sprawled across her bed fully dressed. It appeared that he had just had time to remove his shoes and jacket before crashing out, presumably the worse for drink.

Wearily she sat down on the edge of the bed. It was the last straw. Now it looked as though she'd get no sleep at all. Perhaps if she took a blanket and tried to settle herself on the living-room settee for the few remaining hours. She started to get up, but Adam stirred and threw one arm across her hips, trapping her. Opening one eye, he smiled and lifted his arm to her shoulder to draw her down beside him.

'Oh, it's you,' he murmured into her hair. 'How nice of you to join me. By the way, where have you been?'

She fought him off, frantically beating her fists against his chest. 'Leave me alone. I'm not one of your one-night stands,' she hissed furiously. 'I've been attending to someone who needed me, if you must know.' He released her and she struggled to her feet to stand looking down at him. 'And I'd be grateful if you'd confine your amorous activities to London—at

least until after the divorce.' She turned at the door.
'And *that* can't come soon enough for me.'

She found it impossible to get comfortable on the
settee, let alone to sleep. Her own words echoed
mockingly and insistently on her mind: 'We all need
someone—even the strongest person can't make it
through life in total isolation.' Yet wasn't that exactly
what she was trying to do? Squeezing her eyes shut,
she tried to shut out the picture of Adam's dark eyes
as he looked up at her—the strength of his arms as
they'd tried to pull her close and the warmth of his
cheek against hers. What bliss it would have been to
have given in, a small, traitorous voice goaded, to have
snuggled close and let him make love to you. It's what
you wanted really, didn't you? She clamped her teeth
down hard on to her lower lip. Maybe she would even
have surrendered if she hadn't known that he'd come
straight from another woman's arms. Oh, what have
you got yourself into? she pleaded helplessly. What
kind of man is it that you've married?

Peter wakened her. He looked worried.

'It's half-past seven. I've been trying to wake you for
ages, but you were out for the count.'

She struggled into a sitting position, rubbing her
aching eyes and wincing at the stiffness in her back.
'*Ow*! I must have been lying awkwardly.'

'I'm not surprised. A two-seater settee isn't exactly
the ideal place to spend the night.' Peter cleared his
throat. 'Er—look, tell me to mind my own business if
you like, but is there a particular reason for your being
here?'

'Fleur paged me in the middle of the night,' she told
him hurriedly. 'When I got back it was almost dawn,
and I didn't want to wake everyone.'

'I see. So what time did Adam leave?'

She stared at him. 'Leave? Are you sure?'

'Well, the bedroom door's wide open and empty. The car's gone too.' He frowned. 'You didn't know he was leaving early, then?'

'No.'

Peter shook his head. 'I don't know about you two. It's the strangest marriage I've ever come across. Sometimes I wonder just what *is* going on here.'

Caryn threw aside the blanket and began to get up. 'Oh, for heaven's sake, Pete, nothing's *going on*, as you put it. I expect Adam had a call from London. Maybe there's some emergency. There's probably a note somewhere.' But as she went off to the bathroom she knew there wasn't.

In the kitchen at Wessex House Maggie was busy with breakfast. She looked askance at Caryn as she came in.

'My dear lord, Mrs Laine, you look as though you haven't been to bed all night. But then I don't suppose you did get much rest, did you?'

Caryn looked at her sharply. 'Why do you say that?'

'Well, that terrible crash on the bypass,' Maggie said, breaking eggs into the poacher. 'A real bit of luck, Mr Laine being on the spot, wasn't it?'

Caryn's legs suddenly gave beneath her and she sat down hard on a chair. 'What crash?' she asked stupidly.

'You mean he never told you? Well, isn't that typical? Modest, just like his cousin Dr Michael.' Maggie slipped four more slices of bread into the toaster. 'I heard through the postman,' she said chattily. 'His brother's a policeman and he was on duty last night—at the scene of the crash in seconds, he was.' She sucked in her breath. 'Ghastly sight—bodies all over the road, so he said.'

'Oh, how awful. Anyone killed?' Caryn asked.

'No, thank the Lord. Four badly injured, though, including one little boy. But thanks to Mr Laine being there they all received prompt treatment even before the ambulance arrived. I dare say he saved some lives last night.' Maggie turned to beam at Caryn. 'A real hero, your husband is, Mrs Laine. Aren't you proud of him?'

CHAPTER NINE

CARYN rang Adam's number four times without success. Twice she found herself connected to his answering machine and once his cleaning lady. Finally she tried again at six o'clock, and was relieved when Adam himself answered.

'Adam Laine speaking.' He sounded tired and edgy.

'Adam, it's me, Caryn.'

'Oh—is anything wrong?'

'No—well, *yes*. I'm ringing to apologise—for last night.'

'What in particular about last night?' he asked. His voice was like cold steel, and she swallowed hard.

'I said some—some nasty things—about your being late home. It's really none of my business, and I—I hadn't heard about the accident then.'

'It was nothing. Don't give it another thought.' There was an uncomfortable pause, then, 'Was that all you rang for?'

'Well—yes,' she admitted.

'Is Peter all right?'

'Yes, fine.'

'Good. Look, I shan't be coming down this coming weekend, Caryn. There doesn't seem much point in putting you out. So I'll see you both when Peter's admitted. I've booked you into a hotel quite close to the clinic. I'll send you the details.'

'Oh—thank you.'

'Goodbye, then. See you next week.'

'Goodb——' But before the word was out she heard him hang up. With a sigh she replaced the receiver.

He'd sounded so abrupt and businesslike, almost as though he were talking to a stranger. But then he was. That's what we are, she told herself. Married strangers. She sat staring at the telephone, remembering his words: 'I shan't be coming down. . .there doesn't seem much point in putting you out. I've booked·you into a hotel. . .' A puzzling disappointment assailed her. She'd vaguely thought she might be staying at his flat. Of course, this way was better—much less embarrassing—although. . .

Lisa Gregory arrived late on Friday afternoon, and Caryn took her straight down to the lodge.

˙ She was a small, dynamic woman in her early fifties. Her greying hair was cut short and always looked well groomed, as did the plain tailored clothes that were her hallmark. She always travelled light, so Caryn wasn't surprised to see the small compact suitcase she lifted out of the boot of her car.

'The bare essentials,' she said, seeing Caryn's expression. 'Toothbrush and a change of clothes, that's usually enough.' She gave Caryn a brief hug and looked round. 'Well, I must say you've made a good job of this place. When I first saw it you wouldn't have given tuppence for it.'

'Come through and see the rest. You'll like the kitchen. I'll make you some tea,' said Caryn. 'You must be dying for a cup.'

As always, Lisa made herself instantly at home. Perching on one of the stools at the breakfast bar, she looked out of the window.

'Quite a little Eden, isn't it?' she remarked. 'The new owner must be very grateful to you for doing all this work. I hope he's going to reimburse you adequately.'

Caryn climbed on to the stool opposite. 'The new owner is my husband, Lisa,' she said.

Lisa nodded. 'I know.'

'You know that too? But how, Lisa? Who told you?'

'Your doctor friend Michael Faber wrote and told me. He's very worried about you, so don't think too badly of him. Is it true what he says, Caryn? Did you marry this man just to stay here at Wessex House— and because he thinks he can cure Peter?'

Caryn met Lisa's candid grey eyes squarely. It was pointless trying to manipulate the truth where Lisa was concerned. She always saw straight through any prevaricating. She opened her mouth to own up, then a curious thing happened. She heard herself saying, 'No, Lisa. I married Adam for the time-honoured reason. I love him.' The moment the words were out she felt as though she'd been hit by an avalanche. She'd meant to tell the truth—and now she had.

'Then it's worse than I thought,' sighed Lisa. 'I know about the conditions of his aunt's will, you see. Dr Faber explained all that in his letter too.' She reached across the bar to touch Caryn's hand. 'What were you thinking about, child—marrying a man whose only intention is to use you?'

Caryn swallowed the lump in her throat and forced her voice to remain level. 'Like so many other foolish things, it seemed like a good idea at the time. The perfect solution, in fact.' She shook her head at the older woman. 'Look, Lisa, no one other than Michael knows, and you mustn't breathe a word of this to Peter. His whole future depends on it.'

'But what about *your* future?' Lisa insisted. 'What's going to happen to you? This man—this Adam Laine; does he know how you feel about him?'

Caryn shook her head. 'No, and he mustn't. It's my own bad luck that I've fallen for a hard-headed, self-sufficient businessman. But no one's problem but mine. Once we've fulfilled the conditions of the will we'll divorce and go our own ways. He's planning to make Wessex House into a convalescent home for his wealthy private patients. But he's agreed to let us use part of the building, so that's a plus at least.'

Lisa groaned and bit her lip. 'Oh, Caryn, if only you'd talked to me about this first. I feel partly responsible for it all and now. . .' She took a long drink of her tea and when she looked up again her brow was furrowed. 'Look, love, I said I wanted to talk to you. What I have to tell you is rather bad news—though on reflection maybe it's just as well. . .'

'Please. . .' Caryn smiled ruefully at her. 'I wish you'd tell me.'

'Right. The truth is, I'm going to have to ask you to close the clinic here at Wessex House.'

Caryn's eyes opened wide. '*Close*? Oh, Lisa.'

'I know you've put a lot into the place. And you've spent a lot of your own money on it too—which is why I said I hoped this Laine man would reimburse you. It can't be helped, love. I've racked my brain to try to think of a way, but it can't be done.'

'But why? What's happened?'

'It's our headquarters, Kendal Court,' Lisa told her. 'It's a very old house, as you know, and last winter we had a lot of problems. When we called a builder in he found extensive dry rot. We called in experts and found it was even more serious than I suspected. The upshot is that we need a new roof and various other expensive structural work doing. The only way we can pay for it is to close the two newest clinics—this being one of them.'

Caryn was speechless, and they sat in silence for a moment. 'When I heard that you'd married I was relieved at first,' Lisa went on at last. 'Then I got the letter from Dr Faber and I felt terrible to think that you'd done this crazy thing for us.'

'It was for Peter too,' Caryn explained. 'At least he'll be sure of a good job and a home of his own. He wants to get married, you see, and——'

'*Caryn*!' Lisa interrupted. 'When are you going to think of yourself? What are *you* going to do?'

Caryn smiled wryly. 'Don't think I haven't wondered, but I'm trying hard not to think about that right at this minute,' she said weakly. 'As for the clinic, if it has to close I suppose this is as good a time as any. My three residents are just about ready to leave.'

'I know, and I've been really pleased with the work you and Peter have done here,' said Lisa. 'If it's just you I could offer you a job at Kendal Court again,' she said thoughtfully. 'But frankly, you'd be better off going back into regular nursing. I couldn't afford to pay you what you're worth at the moment.'

Caryn's heart felt like a lead weight in her chest, but she looked up, determined not to let her dismay show. 'Let's not think about it at the moment,' she said. 'Pete and I will be leaving for London on Monday morning. The day after he'll be having his operation. That's about as much as I can handle right now.'

The local paper had got hold of the story about Adam's heroism at the scene of the accident on the bypass. There was even a photograph they had unearthed from somewhere. In the accompanying article Wessex House was named as his 'country residence' and there was a hint about its impending conversion, referring to the new project as a private nursing home. The only reference to Caryn went:

> At present the house is being run as a health farm by Dr Laine's wife, Karen.

Caryn threw down the paper in disgust. Health farm indeed! Where had they got their information? No one had bothered to check with her, and to add insult to injury they'd got just about everything else wrong too.

Caryn and Peter left for London on the early train on the Monday morning. Jilly drove them to the station. She made Caryn promise to ring her the moment the operation was over. As the time for the train's arrival drew near she clung to Peter and, to give them a few moments to themselves, Caryn disappeared to buy magazines at the bookstall.

Peter had flatly refused to take his wheelchair with him to London. 'They'll have plenty at the hospital,' he pointed out, 'and I can just about make it as far as the taxi rank at Waterloo, so why bother?' He grinned with a brave optimism that tugged at Caryn's heart. 'After all, I won't need it on the way home, will I?'

The moment they arrived at the clinic Peter was whisked off to have all his preparatory tests and Caryn, left to her own devices, went off to check into the hotel Adam had booked for her. She found her room with its en-suite bathroom spacious and comfortable. Adam had clearly spared no expense in providing for her comfort. As she began to unpack she wondered whether she would see him before tomorrow.

As it happened, she didn't have to wonder for long. She had just finished putting away the few things she had brought with her when there was a knock on the door. Opening it, she found Adam outside.

'May I come in?' he asked.

'Oh—yes, of course. I'm sorry. I wasn't expecting you.'

He stepped into the room looking puzzled. 'You weren't? Did you think I'd abandon you?'

She flushed. 'No. I just thought you'd be busy, that's all.'

'All my hard work comes tomorrow,' he told her. 'For the moment I'm letting my staff do their share.'

In the awkward silence that followed Caryn racked her brain for something interesting to say. Suddenly she remembered the newspapear article and opened her bag to pull it out.

'Have you seen this?'she asked.

He read it and laughed.

'I'm glad you think it's funny,' she said drily. 'I thought it was awful. Where did they get their information from?'

'Someone rang my secretary, actually,' Adam said indolently.

'And she said I ran a *health farm*?'

'For want of something better to call it,' he said. 'Actually, I thought it was a bit of quick thinking on her part.'

'Did you? It's a pity she didn't think quickly enough to get my name and your title right.'

'Oh, Caryn, what does it matter? It's only a local rag.' He stood up and crossed the room to where she stood by the window. Putting his hands on her shoulders, he found she was trembling.

'Relax—you're all tensed up,' he said quietly. 'Are you worried about Peter?' He turned her round to face him and tipped up her chin with one finger. 'Well, are you?'

'A bit. He is my brother. And it's so desperately important to him.'

'To me too. Can you imagine the responsibility? But I don't suppose you're in the least worried about me?' He drew her gently towards him and searched her face. She looked into the dark eyes and felt as though she were drowning, then suddenly, to her horror and shame, she found herself fighting the tears back.

'Go on,' he said quietly, pulling out a clean white handkerchief. 'Have a good cry—you'll feel better. I'll make myself scarce if you'd rather be alone.'

'No—no.' She took the handkerchief from him. 'I'll be fine in a minute. Don't go, I've got something to tell you—good news.'

He sat down on the bed and drew her down beside him. 'I could do with some good news. Tell me.'

Caryn swallowed her tears, sniffed hard and carefully folded his handkerchief back into its original creases. 'It's just that you'll soon have Wessex House all to yourself. Lisa Gregory's going to have to close our clinic owing to lack of funds.'

Adam stared at her. 'And you call that good news?'

'For you it is. You'll be getting rid of me too. I'm going to have to look for another job. Once you've moved in you can file for divorce as soon as you like.'

He frowned. 'Does Peter know about this?'

'Of course not. I wouldn't dream of telling him until after the operation.' She looked at him anxiously. 'But you will still keep him on as administrator?'

'Naturally.'

Caryn sighed. 'And he and Jilly can still have the lodge?'

'After the work you both put into it I could hardly refuse, could I?'

'That's all right, then.' Caryn stood up and walked away towards the window again. 'I thought I might look round while I'm in London,' she said, 'put out a few feelers. I still have a few contacts. It shouldn't be too difficult to find another job, though I'll miss my work with eating disorders. . .'

'Why not work for me?'

She stopped in mid-sentence to look at him. 'For you?'

He spread his hands. 'I haven't appointed anyone yet to be in charge at Wessex House.'

'Wouldn't that make things rather—well—awkward?'

'Why should it?'

She shook her head. 'The divorce—everything. You won't want me around. Besides, you know how I feel about private treatment.'

'I haven't heard you complaining much about Peter's private treatment,' Adam said drily.

She coloured. 'That's unfair!'

'I know. And I'm sorry.' He grinned. 'I couldn't resist it. There's a certain look about you when you're indignant.'

Her hand went involuntarily to her hair. 'The bronze chrysanthemum syndrome?'

He laughed. 'You remembered.' He stood up and came to her. 'That's better. It's good to see you smile again. Look, no need to make your mind up now, Caryn. Why not sleep on it? I'll tell you what—have a relaxing bath and a rest, then we'll go and see Peter. After that I'll take you to my favourite restaurant for dinner.'

She shook her head. 'It's all right, Adam, you don't have to feel responsible for me. I've got a good book, and an early night will do me good.'

'Are you saying you'd rather not have dinner with me?'

She shook her head. 'I'm sure there must be something else you'd rather do.'

'Perhaps you'd like to let me be the judge of that.'

'Well, if it's really not putting you out.'

'Caryn, we *are* married.'

'On paper.'

'Whose fault is that?'

She turned away. 'I married you to fulfil the conditions of your aunt's will. I never agreed to anything else.'

Adam looked at her for a long minute, then lifted his shoulders helplessly. 'You're right, you didn't. And you never lose an opportunity to make that clear. But I think we should try to put on some kind of show of normality, don't you? If only for Peter's sake.' He headed for the door. 'I'll pick you up in an hour—right?'

She turned to reply, but the door was already closing behind him.

Peter was settled in his room at the clinic and looking very comfortable.

'I've got my own television with remote control,' he said, demonstrating by switching channels. 'And the prettiest nurses you've ever seen.' He grinned at Adam. 'Where do you find them?'

'You'd better not let Jilly hear you,' Adam warned, laughing. 'You're supposed to be all pale and suffering nobly.'

'I'll be that tomorrow,' Peter promised. 'I'm hoping to use my temporary fragility to stash up points for later on.' He grinned at Caryn. 'Only joking, Sis.'

Caryn smiled back, but she wasn't fooled. She could see beyond the cheeky smile to the the apprehension lurking in his eyes, and the tiny tension lines at the corners of his mouth. She felt her throat tighten.

In the lift on the way down, she turned to Adam. 'He will be all right, won't he?' she asked anxiously.

He slipped an arm around her shoulders. 'I promise you he will.'

'You can't promise. I'm a nurse, don't forget, I know

the risks involved.' She looked up at him quickly. 'Oh, I know you'll do your best.'

'You're very kind,' he said drily.

'I'm sorry. It's just that Peter is all the family I've got. We've always been very close. If anything happened. . .'

'It *won't*. As you say, you're a nurse, so you know how slim the odds are against anything going wrong. . .' He raised an eyebrow at her. 'Particularly with my kind of genius.' The lift stopped and they got out. The girl at the reception desk smiled and said good evening to Adam, and, although Caryn didn't notice, cast a speculative eye over her. All the staff had been wondering what kind of girl had finally captured the heart of the elusive Adam Laine.

The restaurant Adam had chosen was small, comfortable and discreet. The food and wine were delicious, and Adam chose for her from the menu, recommending the lightest dishes to tempt her depleted appetite. But Caryn couldn't do justice to any of it. She picked at the food, trying hard to appear appreciative and keep up the conversation. At last Adam said, 'I'm taking you back to the hotel now. I think you should try to get a good night's rest.'

In the car she was silent. She protested weakly when Adam said he would see her to her room, but when he ignored her protests she didn't argue. Taking the key from her, he opened the door. Inside she gave a sigh of relief.

'I'm sorry,' he said.

'What for?'

'It was a mistake, taking you to dinner, wasn't it? I should have listened when you said you didn't want to go.' He looked at her. 'You always say what you mean, don't you, Caryn? It's unusual in a woman. But then I'm learning that there's a lot about you that's unusual.'

'Oh, surely not.'

'Oh, it's true. But you don't want to hear about that now.'

He turned to go, and Caryn felt panic rise suffocatingly in her chest. Suddenly she didn't want to be left alone—alone to think, about Peter and his operation—about the failure of the project they had invested so much hope in—but mainly about the emotional madness she had allowed herself to become enmeshed in that was causing her so much pain.

'Don't go, Adam,' she said suddenly as he reached the door. 'I feel more relaxed here. I can make you some coffee if you like. Look, there's a machine—everything we need.'

He paused, his hand on the door-handle. 'All right, if you let me send down for some brandy. I think you need it.' He glanced hesitantly at her. 'You're sure you want me to stay?'

'I'm sure.'

When the brandy arrived Adam poured a large measure into Caryn's coffee, and as she drank and the warmth spread through her she relaxed visibly. It also began to loosen her tongue and she kept up a constant flow of chatter—about Wessex House and her clients, about Peter and their childhood escapades; anything and everything to delay the inevitable moment when he would leave and she would be alone with her own unwelcome thoughts. Finally he reached out to touch her hand.

'Caryn—look, like it or not, I'm not leaving you like this. Go and get ready for bed. Do you have any sleeping tablets?'

She stared at him with enormous eyes. 'No.'

'Well, it can't be helped. Perhaps the brandy will make you sleep.' He smiled wryly at her sudden hesitation. 'Don't worry, I'll make myself comfortable in a chair and stay till you're asleep.'

'You can't do that, Adam. I won't let you,' she said earnestly. 'You have a heavy day ahead of you tomorrow. You need your rest too.'

He smiled. 'Well, we'll play it by ear, shall we?'

In the bathroom she undressed and put on her nightdress and dressing-gown then she came back to slip into the king-sized bed that Adam had turned down for her. He'd been right about the brandy; it had made her feel pleasantly drowsy and relaxed. He drew up a chair at the foot of the bed.

'I'll put the light off and you can talk or sleep, whatever makes you feel better.'

She yawned, grateful for the luxurious feel of the soft mattress and silky sheets. 'You're being very good to me,' she said. 'I haven't been very nice to you, have I?'

'I daresay you reacted in exactly the way I deserved,' he said wryly.

As her eyes became accustomed to the dim light she could make out the outline of his profile. Suddenly he felt like someone she had known for a very long time. 'Please, Adam,' she said, 'I wish you'd get some rest yourself. Look, it's a huge bed. Why don't you take off your shoes and lie down?'

He smiled. 'If you were any other girl that invitation might be taken the wrong way. If only I didn't know that you're only suggesting it because you're afraid I might fall asleep in the middle of Peter's operation tomorrow.' Nevertheless, a moment later she felt the mattress dip as he stretched out his long length on the other side of the huge bed.

For several minutes there was silence and Caryn wondered whether he had fallen asleep. She raised herself on one elbow to look at him, but his eyes were wide open, staring at the ceiling. He turned his head on the pillow to look at her, his eyes twinkling.

'"Well, this is a fine mess you've got me into, Stanley"', he joked.

'Is it?'

His lips curved with amusement. 'To coin a phrase—if my friends could see me now. Caryn. . .'

'Yes?'

'Feeling better?'

'Much.' She lay back against the pillow again.

'I wonder if you know how much I envy you,' Adam said softly.

'You—envy *me*?' she said incredulously.

'Oh, yes.'

'Whatever do I have for you to envy?'

'You have someone to care for—who cares for you in return. That's something I never had in all my life.'

She felt the breath catch in her throat. This wasn't the Adam Laine that Michael, his own cousin, had painted for her. 'I thought you were self-sufficient,' she said. 'And you did have your aunt Grace. She cared about you.'

'She felt *responsible* for me,' he corrected. 'That's not at all the same thing. For years I thought I had everything—that I didn't need people. But that was before. . .' He turned to look at her. 'Seeing Peter and you together—especially this afternoon, I saw something I've never experienced for myself. You care as much about him as you do about yourself—more, perhaps. You've sacrificed so much for him.'

'He deserves it,' she said simply. 'He's had some very bad luck. He'd have done it all for me if it had been the other way around.'

'I believe it.'

She turned to meet his eyes and saw them shining in the darkness.

'Shall I tell you something?' he said. 'It made me feel ashamed.'

'Of what?' she queried.

'Of my selfishness in asking you to marry me.'

There was a moment's pause, then she said, 'You wanted the house. It was yours by right and you had plans for it. Besides, I could always have said no.'

'And now, losing your clinic—to find you did it all for nothing. That must have been a bitter blow. If you took the job I offered you, you could still do your own work, you know—still have a few clients of your own to treat.'

While they had been talking, each without the other's knowledge had been reaching out across the empty stretch of bed between them. Suddenly their fingertips touched and curled around each other. Caryn felt a lump fill her throat.

'Thank you, Adam,' she whispered. 'And you're wrong in one thing. It wasn't just for the sake of the clinic that I agreed to your proposal.'

'You mean what I'm doing for Peter?' he said. 'Forget that. It's my job.'

'I wasn't thinking of Peter,' she said.

'You weren't?'

'No.'

He moved closer, propping himself on one elbow and leaning over her to look into her eyes. 'Then you don't hate me?'

'It's said that hate can be very close to love,' she said drowsily.

'Would you care to endorse that point?'

Her heart began to drum, stirring her blood to a heady exhilaration, and she reached up to wind her arms around his neck. The next moment his lips were on hers. He kissed her, gently at first, then hungrily, his hands cradling her head. When he gently parted her lips with his tongue she responded passionately, moving closer to him, and was faintly surprised to find herself undoing the buttons of his shirt and helping him off with it. A few minutes later he slid between the sheets next to her and took her in his arms.

'This is the first time I've really felt you wanted me,' he whispered, caressing her tenderly. His eyes smiled whimsically into hers. 'You're not going to ask me to leave now, are you? Because I warn you, I might ignore the request this time.'

For answer she reached out to hold him close, burying her face against his shoulder. 'Of couse I'm not going to ask you to leave,' she whispered against the corner of his mouth. 'I don't want you to go away ever again.'

When she awakened the sunlight was streaming into the room. She was alone and, as she lay in the big bed in the strange hotel room, she thought for a moment that she must have dreamed the whole thing. Then she saw the note propped against the bedside lamp. Opening it, she read:

> You looked so peaceful that I hadn't the heart to wake you. Thank you for last night, darling. See you later, Adam.

Caryn sat up in bed, one hand to her forehead, frowning with the effort of remembering. Last night— she knew they'd slept together, but how—and why had it all come about? She remembered making coffee— Adam had sent down for brandy. She must have been slightly tipsy, but not so tipsy that she couldn't remember what had happened between them. 'Thank you for last night, darling.' Her cheeks flamed when she remembered the touch of his hand—his lips. And her own uninhibited—no, *fevered* response to his love-making. It wasn't fair. She'd been tired and over-wrought—the brandy had gone straight to her head, or she would never. . . Nothing had really changed between them. Their marriage could never work. They came from different worlds, their values were totally opposite. But Adam had won. She'd given in and let him—no, *invited* him to make love to her. She sighed. And now—although he would never know it—nothing would ever be the same again.

Suddenly she remembered that this was the day of Peter's operation and felt ashamed. Her first thoughts should have been of him. She rang down for coffee and toast, got out of bed, showered and dressed, then sat down to eat a sketchy breakfast.

At the clinic she learned that Peter was already in theatre. I should have been here to reassure him, she reproached herself. Seeing her anguish, the nurse assured her that he'd been too drowsy from his pre-med to notice her absence.

'Why not look round the West End shops?' she suggested. 'Your brother will be in surgery for some hours and unfit to see you for a while after that. Waiting around here will only make you tense.'

So Caryn went out into the warm summer morning. She walked through Mayfair to join the bustle of shoppers in Regent Street, trying to interest herself in the shop-window displays, her thoughts divided between Peter and Adam.

The hours seemed to drag interminably. She drank coffee she didn't want, looked unseeingly at clothes she had little interest in and occupied an hour picking her way through a lunch she had no appetite for. Finally, when it was time to start back to the clinic, it was all she could do to walk. Everything in her wanted to run back to the hospital.

The sister on Peter's ward told her that he was still

sleeping and that the operation had been successful. She was to be allowed to sit with him for a while. A nurse took her to his room and left her there alone.

He looked peaceful, almost like a little boy again. Caryn sat down by the bed and watched him, wondering if he would wake before she left so that she could reassure herself that he was really all right. Presently the door opened softly and she looked up to see Adam standing at the foot of the bed. He smiled at her.

'Everything went well, Caryn,' he told her quietly. 'There were no complications and he should make a full recovery.'

'Thank you, Adam. I'm very grateful—more than I can ever say. We can never hope to repay you.'

His eyes clouded. 'I told you, it's my job.' He raised her to her feet, his hands under her elbows. 'Caryn, what is it?' He searched her eyes. 'You're regretting last night?'

'Yes—but I can't talk—not here.'

He glanced at Peter. 'I think you should leave now anyway. He won't wake for a while. You can come back this evening.'

With one last reluctant glance at Peter, she allowed herself to be led out of the room. In the corridor Adam looked at her. 'Come back to the flat with me?' As he saw her hesitation his eyes flashed with irritation. 'For heaven's sake, Caryn! We obviously need to talk. We can't do it in a corridor.'

His flat was as she had always imagined—sleek, expensive and unlived-in. She perched uneasily on the edge of a chair while he made coffee.

'Right,' he said briskly, putting the tray down on the coffee table, 'tell me what's worrying you.'

'Do you really have to ask?'

'At the risk of being thought unimaginative, yes, I do.'

'It shouldn't have happened, Adam. I was tired and over-emotional, and the brandy went straight to my head.'

'Are you accusing me of something?' he demanded.

She coloured and avoided his burning eyes. 'No. And I'm not making excuses either.'

'Then *what* for heaven's sake?'

Caryn took a deep breath. 'I think we should get a divorce as soon as possible,' she said hurriedly. 'Staying married is just making things worse. It's served the purpose it was designed for. You've more than adequately repaid me for falling in with your plans. Continuing this charade is just going to make life complicated for both of us.'

'*Charade*?' Adam stared at her. 'I don't understand any of this. I thought we'd come to a new understanding.'

She shook her head. 'It would never work, Adam. Marriage is more than physical attraction. We're from different worlds. We think differently. We don't want the same things from life.'

There was a moment's pause, then he said, 'Would you care to tell me in what way you feel our wants differ?'

She licked her dry lips. 'You see life as a series of material challenges. You need to make money—to have people look up to you—to be admired and respected.'

'Is that so bad?'

'Not bad. Just—not the way *I* see things. I happen to feel that *people* are more important than money. I think that very often people deserve more than simply what they can pay for in hard cash.'

'You don't feel that it's possible for the people who *can* pay to help those who can't?'

She stared at him. 'I don't understand. . .'

Adam got to his feet. 'There are a whole lot of things you don't understand, Caryn,' he said, his eyes dark. 'And you don't seem inclined to give me the benefit of the doubt.' He stood up suddenly. 'Come on, I'm taking you to see something.' Hardly giving her time to put down her cup, he grasped her arm and strode out of the flat, hustling her along with him.

The traffic was heavy and they had been driving eastwards for about forty minutes when Adam pulled up outside a row of dingy houses in the East End. Without a word he opened the door and got out. Caryn followed. Holding her arm firmly, he walked up the steps of a crumbling three-storey Victorian house and walked in. A smiling woman in a blue uniform came to meet him.

'Mr Laine, this is a nice surprise. The children will be pleased to see you. Can you stay for tea?'

'Yes, please, Sister. I've brought my wife to meet you all. Caryn, this is Sister Frances.'

The woman turned to smile at Caryn, holding out her hand. 'How nice to meet you, Mrs Laine. We've all been looking forward to meeting you. Do come and say hello to the children.'

She led them through to a room at the back where long windows opened on to a small garden. About twenty children played on a patch of scrubby grass in the shade of a few dusty trees. Some were pitifully disabled. Caryn turned shocked, enquiring eyes up to Adam.

'Most of them are orphans,' he told her quietly. 'Some are from Third World Countries—a few from Romania and Lithuania. What they have in common is that they all arrived in dire need of medical help and none have anyone to care for them. This is Grace Laine House. The Mayfair clinic is run solely to finance it, but over the last couple of years we've been finding it hard to make ends meet—which is why I want to move them all to Wessex House. Apart from anything else they can have fresh air and a healthier life there.' He looked at her. 'These are the "wealthy patients" you've been visualising, Caryn. They're all the family I have, and when I offered you a job I hoped you might help me care for them.'

When the children saw him they flocked around him, all laughing and chattering at once as they competed for his attention. Heedless of his clothes, he sat down on the grass, letting them hug him and climb all over him. Sister Frances smiled at Caryn.

'He's so good with them. Many of them would be dead by now if it weren't for him. They all love him very much.'

In the car on the way back to the flat Caryn said, 'Why didn't you tell me about Grace Laine house and the children, Adam? Why did you let me go on thinking of you as selfish and hard?'

'It seemed that was what you wanted to think about me,' he said. 'There was no reason why I should tell you. Very few people know, actually.'

'Does Mike know?'

He shook his head. 'Mike and I had very little to do with each other until Aunt Grace died. He's another one who chooses to think the worst of me.' He looked at his watch. 'Well, I suppose I can live with it. I expect you'd like to go straight to the clinic to see Peter. I'll drop you off on the way.'

'Thank you.' Caryn glanced at him. Much as she wanted to see Peter, she felt it was important to talk things through with Adam—to work out their misunderstanding. Suddenly she felt badly in the wrong. 'I'm sorry, Adam,' she said inadequately. 'I'd really like. . .'

'No need,' he said abruptly. 'It was a piece of self-indulgence, taking you to Grace Laine House today. Perhaps it was unfair of me to do it. I realise that it can't make any difference to the way you feel.'

She turned to him. 'But it does, Adam, now that I know. It makes *all* the——'

'Ah, here we are,' Adam interrupted, stopping the car. 'I'm afraid I'll have to ask you to get out quickly—I'm on a double yellow line.' He leaned over to kiss her cheek briefly. 'Goodbye, Caryn, and thanks for all you've done to help me. I'm sorry it had to end like this.'

As she stood on the pavement, watching the car drive away, the word *goodbye* rang in her mind with a terrible finality.

CHAPTER TEN

PETER progressed rapidly. Within a few days he was getting up for short periods, going for short, gentle walks along the corridor and beginning his daily physiotherapy sessions. Caryn spent every afternoon with him, but at last it was time for her to say goodbye and return to Dorset.

On her last afternoon she sat with Peter on the balcony of his room, taking tea in the sunshine.

'What's up?' asked Peter. 'You haven't been looking your usual self these last few days.'

'I'm fine,' she protested.

'No, you're not. You can't fool me,' he said abruptly. 'I'm going to miss you when you've gone. If there's anything worrying you why don't you get it off your chest before you go?'

'You don't want to hear about my problems. Just concentrate on getting strong again. As for missing me. . .' She smiled at him. 'Jilly's coming up to spend a few days with you tomorrow. You can start making plans now. You won't miss me in the least, and you know it.'

'That's not true.' He caught at her hand, his eyes serious. 'Caryn, don't think I don't realise what you've sacrificed for me.' He shook her hand, making her look at him. 'It's Adam, isn't it? He looks fed up too. And you haven't been to see me together once.'

'He's busy. His hours. . .'

'Rubbish. Tell me what's wrong. Have you quarrelled?'

182

'It was my fault,' she said miserably. 'But it's a long story. You don't want to hear. . .'

'But I *do*,' he interrupted. 'I don't know what you've been up to, but I want to hear all about it—*now*, if you don't mind.'

Reluctantly Caryn poured out the whole story to him. He would need to know about the closure of the Gregory Clinic anyway, and if the divorce was going ahead it wouldn't be long before he found out that her marriage to Adam had been a business arrangement. As she unfolded the story to him his eyes grew wider and wider.

'I can't believe I'm *hearing* this,' he said incredulously. 'If it wasn't so bizarre I'd suspect you were pulling my leg.'

'Adam wants you to stay on as his administrator,' she assured him. 'It's a very worthwhile job, Peter. I'm sure you'll be happy. And you and Jilly can live in the lodge.'

'Never mind all that. What about you?' Peter persisted.

'Oh, he offered me a job too, but in the circumstances I can't take it. I'll soon get another job, don't worry. I——'

'Caryn, it's your emotional state I'm talking about. Don't tell me you don't love Adam, because you do—it's written all over you. And I'd stake my life on it that he feels the same way about you.' She was silent, and he went on, 'Oh, Caryn, what a mess you've got yourself into! What you two have done to each other is nothing short of emotional vandalism.'

In the silence that followed she raised her eyes to meet his. 'What am I going to do, Pete?' she asked him miserably. 'I misjudged him so badly.'

He leaned forward to pat her shoulder. 'Have you tried talking to him?'

'Yes.'

'And?'

'He gave me the impression that he didn't want to know.'

He pursed his lips. 'Mmm, can't say I'm surprised. You seem to have taken it for granted that he was a grade A rat from the start. And you can both take full marks for stubborn pride. Why don't you just let things ride for a while? It'll all come right in the end, you'll see.'

And though Caryn could see no solution to the problem she nodded cheerfully and made herself smile at him as she stood up to leave. 'You just behave yourself and do what the nurses tell you,' she warned. 'And take it easy. No sliding down the banisters or entering yourself for the London Marathon at least until next week, anyway!'

She didn't see Adam before she left for Dorset. She'd wondered hopefully if she might run into him on one of her visits to the clinic, but she didn't. Screwing up all her courage, she telephoned his flat on her last evening, but she got the answering machine again. She hung up without leaving a message, almost relieved. After all, what could she say?

Back at Wessex House everything seemed to be winding down. Fleur was ready to leave. She'd been taken to see the restaurant the previous weekend, and she was full of enthusiasm, especially over the flat where she, Fred and Annie would live as a family.

Sarah too was planning her return home with enthusiasm. She and her husband Bob were to have a holiday. A friend had offered to have the children for a week so that they could get away alone.

'It'll be like a second honeymoon,' she told Caryn. 'I can't tell you how wonderful Bob's been about all this.'

The word *honeymoon* raised all kinds of images in Caryn's mind, but she forced herself not to think about them. It was over between her and Adam. There were times when she wished she had never met him—*almost*.

Helen was the only one who still had no plans for leaving. Caryn guessed she still felt a little insecure about going out into the community again, and she asked Lisa if she would take her back to Yorkshire with her. Lisa agreed to let her help out there for a small wage until she was able to live on her own again.

By the following Saturday Caryn had Wessex House to herself. After the excited preparation, packing and goodbyes a feeling of anticlimax descended on her, and to dispel the sudden loneliness she helped Maggie clean all the vacated rooms. But when lunchtime came and the housekeepr had gone home the moment she had dreaded arrived. She stood alone in the wide hallway of the silent, empty house, feeling more alone than she had ever felt in her life. The project she and Peter had put so much into was gone. Soon he wouldn't need her any more. It seemed that her skills as a therapist and counsellor were no longer in demand, and soon her marriage—if one could call it that—would be over too. She felt tears of self-pity begin to prick her eyelids and gave herself an admonishing shake.

'This won't do. Pull yourself together,' she told herself sternly. Gardening—that always worked. Hard physical work never failed to put things in their proper perspective.

Changing into tattered jeans and an ancient shirt, she collected the implements from the potting shed and set about the work with vigour. There was no one waiting for her time or attention. She could work till it was dark if she chose; until she was too tired to think any more.

Over the past few weeks the weeds had been growing

fast and there was plenty for her to do. She was
applying herself to it so energetically that she didn't
hear a step on the path or even at first hear the voice
that quietly spoke her name.

'Caryn.'

She went on digging.

'*Caryn*'.

She stopped to look up, her face flushed and her hair
standing on end. Her heart almost stopped beating.
'*Adam*.' Her hand went involuntarily to her hair, but
he stepped forward to stop her.

'Don't. I like it just like that.'

'I—I wasn't expecting anyone.' She wiped her grimy
hands down the front of her shirt. 'I must look a mess.'

'You look wonderful to me.' His eyes were tender.
'More like a bronze chrysanthemum than ever. Oh,
Caryn, we've been such fools!' He reached out for her,
but she stepped backwards.

'I'm filthy—I'll ruin your suit.'

'To hell with the suit.' He pulled her to him and held
her close, kissing her till she gasped for breath. For a
moment she held her arms rigidly, then, in surrender,
she allowed them to creep around his neck, kissing him
back with all the longing she had tried so hard to
suppress.

'You smell lovely,' he murmured against her hair.
'Of fresh air and earth and blossom and everything
that's wholesome. I love you, Caryn. And I *won't* let
you go. I want you to be my wife, do you understand?'

She looked up at him, her eyes shining. 'I *am* your
wife.'

'Not yet. Not properly. Not the way I want you to
be. I know you love me too, Caryn, even though
you've never said so. Peter told me——'

'*Peter*? That brother of mine. . .'

'That brother of yours has more sense than the two

of us put together,' said Adam. 'Now, Mrs Laine, will you kindly put away that spade and come with me?'

'Kindly don't order me about,' she said, her voice light with laughter. 'Give me one good reason why I should jump just because you tell me to.'

He grasped her shoulders and kissed her hard. 'That's *one* good reason,' he told her. 'And another is that I don't want to have to make love to you out here with all the wildlife looking on.'

They walked towards the house, arms around each other, Caryn in her tattered jeans and Adam in his city suit. On the steps of the house he stopped and looked at her.

'Before we go in I want to hear you say it, please.'

'Say what?'

'Do you want to drive me mad, woman?' He took a step backwards. 'Or do you want me to turn round and drive straight back to London?'

Laughing, she reached out for him. 'No, no, I'll say it.' Standing on the step above him so that their eyes were level, she rested her hands on his shoulders. 'I love you, Adam. I always have.'

He closed the space between them and cupped her face with his hands. 'Me too. I couldn't have married you without. I let you go on thinking badly of me. I thought it might make it easier for us both when the time came to say goodbye.'

She looked at him. 'Oh, Adam, if you only *knew* how it hurt when I thought I'd lost you.' Winding her arms around his neck, she kissed him. After a moment he bent to scoop her up and carry her in through the front door of Wessex House. In the hall, as he shouldered the door shut, he paused to look down at her, his eyes suddenly dancing with laughter.

'What is it?' she asked. 'What's amusing you?'

'I was just thinking of Aunt Grace,' he said, chuckling. 'When she stipulated that I live here with my wife and children, I bet she didn't visualise twenty of them, all at one go.' He shook his head. 'She's got her way after all, bless her. I've a feeling she knew what she was doing when she made that codicil. Maybe she cared more about me than I realised.'

'Maybe she did at that,' Caryn agreed. And as they started to go upstairs she said her own silent 'thank you' to Aunt Grace.

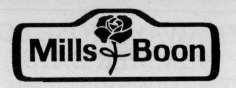

— *MEDICAL* /\ *ROMANCE* —

The books for enjoyment this month are:

THE CALL OF LOVE Jenny Ashe
A HEART UNTAMED Judith Worthy
WAITING GAME Laura MacDonald
THE WESSEX SUMMER Sarah Franklin

♥   ♥   ♥   ♥   ♥

Treats in store!

Watch next month for the following absorbing stories:

SURGEON OF THE HEART Sharon Wirdnam
A GENTLE GIANT Caroline Anderson
DREAM OF NAPLES Lisa Cooper
HAND IN HAND Margaret Barker